"We're going to do this ceremony," she said. "It'll make us like sisters, and it'll make you one of us."

She began to chant, raising her hands to the ceiling. In the eerie light, it was pretty weird. I had never seen anyone in a trance before. Maybe I was kind of in a trance, too, because I imagined the room slipping away from us. It almost felt as if we had been transported to the outback, the home of her people.

I watched, spellbound, as Mick drew lines on her face and arms with a lump of clay. Then, she reached over and drew matching lines on my face and arms. All the while, she sang softly. Then suddenly, I noticed that the tune had changed. She sang a line in her aborigine language and then paused, as if she were waiting for someone to repeat the line.

I realized that someone was me.

DANGER
DOWN UNDER

by Cindy Savage

Cover illustration by Richard Kriegler

*To my hiking and story-telling buddies
at Fleming Girl Scout Camp. May you
have many more great adventures!*

Published by Willowisp Press, Inc.
10100 SBF Drive, Pinellas Park, FL 34666

Text copyright © 1992 by Cindy Savage
Cover copyright © 1992 by Willowisp Press, Inc.

Printed in the United States of America

2 4 6 8 10 9 7 5 3 1

ISBN 0-87406-589-5

Contents

CHAPTER ONE
Can People Melt?

I stared out the window of the small, two-engine commuter airplane as we circled the Adelaide airport. There below me was the place I had been wondering about for years, the place that had fascinated me ever since I got my pen pal. I couldn't believe that down there were all the things I'd read about for so long—wallabies, platypuses, dingoes, the huge desert outback, millions of sheep, and, of course, kangaroos! It seemed unreal, but I was finally there.

Maybe I'd better slow down a little. I'm Dusty Martin, a normal 15-year-old girl from New York. A few years ago, I had an English project in school where I got a pen pal from Australia. At first, I wasn't too into it. But it turned out that my pen pal and I got to be pretty good friends—even though we had never met. And now we were going to meet, just as soon as the plane touched down.

But now that I was about to step off the plane in exotic Australia, it was actually about the last place on earth I wanted to be. It might sound kind of strange that I wasn't too happy about being there, but I can explain.

I had been taking flying lessons in New York. I was learning how to pilot a plane, and I was really close to starting the advanced class. Then I had to stop and come to Australia. I had signed up for the trip a while back, and I couldn't change it. I really loved my flying lessons. But now they would have to wait.

Sure, I was excited about meeting my pen pal after all these years and seeing Australia. But I just couldn't get into it the way I thought I would. Maybe it had something to do with the other thing that was happening to me.

To take my mind off of how depressed I was, I imagined flying the plane I was on. I was in position, heading into the wind. I could see the airport shimmering in the afternoon heat up ahead. The plane shuddered as it descended through the layer of heat rising off the runway. I got my instructions from the tower.

Mentally I ran through the landing checklist. *Flaps up. Landing gear down.* The engines whined as they reduced speed. *Pull up the nose. Set it down gently. Apply the brakes.* I loved the feeling of power as the plane thundered down the runway toward the terminal.

I almost felt as if I were at the stick.

My imagination steered the plane toward the ground terminal. I had steered a similar course at different airports back home with my instructor as I worked toward my private pilot's license.

And, I told myself, when all the passengers had gotten off, I'd refuel, signal the tower again and zoom off into the blue sky.

I would, that is, if I weren't stuck for three months on a continent smack-dab in the middle of the ocean.

I must have looked pretty unhappy because the woman sitting next to me said, "Don't look so glum, Dusty. You'll love Australia. Just give it a little time."

She was pretty nice. I had talked to her a little when I wasn't daydreaming about being home, flying an airplane. She told me her name was Nancy. "Give it a little time," I repeated. "All I have is time. Three months of time to kill before the baby's born, and then life as I know it will cease to exist."

That was the other complication in my life.

I was going to get a new baby brother. At my age! At my parents' age! I mean, I *like* being the only kid. And I thought my mom and dad *liked* just having me. Anyway, there were going to be big, big changes at home with the new baby around. And I wasn't looking forward to them!

Nancy laughed. "Somehow, I think all of this talk of gloom and doom is stretching it a bit." I had told her a little about what was bugging me. "A new baby brother could be nice. He'll look up to you—his big sister. Believe me. And in the meantime, you have this great chance to explore a new country."

I sighed and stared out the window.

She tried again. "The openness will grow on you, Dusty. The history and customs will creep into your subconscious mind and change you forever. Wait and see."

Nancy was nice, but she was a little weird. I guess she was really into Australia. I knew she was hoping I would smile, but I just didn't feel like it. Once again, I wished I had got my license before I left New York. Now I wouldn't get to fly again until I was back in the States. And then, my parents probably wouldn't have time to run me to the airport. They would be too busy with the new baby!

"Well, we're here," Nancy said as the *Fas-*

ten Seat Belts sign blinked off. "And just think," she added. "You're here during a very unusual time. I hear there has never been a December this hot."

"Great," I muttered sarcastically as I followed her down the steps and off the plane. "December is supposed to be cold—Christmas, winter, lots of snow!"

"Have a great summer," she called to me as she walked to the terminal.

I waved and smiled. I knew she was just trying to cheer me up. I had almost forgotten that the seasons are reversed in Australia because it's in the Southern Hemisphere. That was *another* thing I had to get used to!

Stepping off the plane was like walking into a blast furnace. *Can people melt?* I wondered. At home it was freezing. Here it was the hottest summer that southern Australia had ever had. And to top it all off, I had to go to an Australian school with my pen pal after Christmas!

Suddenly, I heard someone call to me. "Dusty! Hey, sister, over here!" A girl waved at me frantically from the open door of the terminal. "Come on, mate. You're going to be a lobster before you get under cover!"

I recognized her from the picture she'd sent. She was shorter than I was, and had black

11

curly hair and brown skin. She was an aborigine, the original people who lived in Australia before the Europeans came in the 1700s—sort of like Native Americans in the United States.

"Hi, you must be Michelle," I said, reaching out my hand. She slapped it.

"Call me Mick, mate," she said. "Michelle's way too long in this kind of weather!"

"Mick?" I asked. "Like in 'Crocodile Dundee'?"

"Right-o! The very same. Lot of us blokes named Mick down under."

Mick's Aussie accent and lingo took a little getting used to. "By 'down under' you mean in Australia, right?"

"You got it, mate!" Mick skipped ahead of me down toward the luggage carousel. Her quick movements and cheery conversation were too much after the long trip from New York, 26 hours of flying, not to mention the half-day layover in Tokyo. My head ached. The hot air was hard to breathe. It was going to be a long winter—oops, I mean summer.

I caught a glimpse of Nancy again, as she bent down to get her luggage—a battered army duffel bag with world travel patches all over it. She flashed me a thumbs-up sign and then disappeared into the crowd.

"Come on, mate," Michelle—I mean Mick—said when we had picked up my luggage. "Let's get a taxi."

"Didn't your parents come?" I asked.

"They're at home. They thought the two of us would have better luck fighting the airport crush this *arvo* without them."

"This *arvo*?" I asked.

"You know, this afternoon," Mick replied.

"Oh—*arvo*—afternoon. Uhh, I get it."

"Glad you're here, mate," Mick said when we were walking outside to wait for the taxi. "Got a lot of things planned. We'll go to the wallaby races and try our hand at sheep shearing. We'll pop some honeypots at the *billabong*—that means to make big splashes at the swimming pool, you know. We'll do some scuba diving, fishing, the works. After you get a good night's sleep of course."

"I'm fine, really," I said, dragging my feet after her. "Air travel doesn't bother me a bit." I yawned.

"Hey! Watch out!" Mick said, suddenly nudging me out of the way. She had barely pushed me, but I stumbled and landed on my rear. I sat there on the sidewalk, looking up at her concerned face.

"What's wrong, Mick?" I asked. I didn't see anything.

"Sorry, mate," she said, helping me up. "But you almost stepped on a red ant. For me, that's like killing a relative."

"Huh?" I asked, brushing red dust off of my jeans. Was she nuts? I stared at her. "I know most people have *aunts* for relatives, but *ants*?" I guessed that maybe Mick had waited for me out in the sun too long, and her brain had fried.

But Mick's grin returned. "Come on. Here's the taxi. Get in and I'll explain."

"This better be good," I said as I carefully stepped over the line of little red ants on the ground in front of the taxi. "Excuse me, *Ant* Minnie," I said, looking down at them.

When we were in the taxi, Mick explained. "All aborigines have a dreamtime ancestor. Dreamtime is the time before people existed on the earth. Before we are even born, we belong to a totem clan. My totem is the red ant. I'm related to all of the red ants that ever were or ever will be. My grandfather taught me a songline that proves it."

"Proves what?"

"That mine is a red ant dreaming."

"Oh." I couldn't tell if she was serious or not. As tired as I was, it sure sounded like a lot of mumbo jumbo to me. My eyes grew heavy as Mick went on. My headache had

14

gotten worse.

"My soul is eternally linked with the red ant and the dreaming tracks that it followed," Mick explained. "So, I can't kill my relatives, can I?"

"I guess not," I mumbled sleepily.

Dreamtime? Songline? Dreaming tracks? I decided Mick's brain was definitely frazzled by the heat. I laid my head back on the seat and tried to will my headache away. Instead, when I closed my eyes, all I saw were the faces of my parents as they told me the news.

"We're going to have a baby, Dusty," Mom had said. *"The doctor already says it will be a boy. He'll come in the spring."*

"A baby? You have to be kidding! I thought I was going to be your only kid?" I had whined.

"We thought so, too," Dad said. *"But now we're going to have the family we've always wanted—a boy and a girl!"*

Then the next thing I knew, I was off to Australia for the student exchange program that I had signed up for almost a year earlier. I was going to live with Mick's family for three months this year. Then Mick was going to come to our house next fall. It had sounded like fun at the time. But the new baby brother meant big changes. My video game and computer room would be turned into a nursery. And I was sure my parents were going to be more interested in decorating the baby's room than in paying for flying lessons for me.

I tried to back out of the exchange trip, but Mom and Dad thought I should go. So while they were getting ready for this new baby, I was sent halfway around the world to bake in the sun.

It was almost as if they had wanted me out of the way. I know they really loved me, but it still wasn't fair.

CHAPTER TWO
The Legend Of Wild Joe

I drifted in and out of sleep as the cab drove through the city of Adelaide. Mick's voice faded in and out as she pointed out the different sights in the town. She asked me a few questions about America and New York, but she must have noticed I was zonked out and stopped talking.

After I don't know how long, I heard her say, "We're here!"

I opened my eyes to see that we had stopped in front of a nice limestone and brick, single-story house. It looked a lot like an American house. Mick paid the cab driver and leaped out of the car. As I climbed out, I noticed our reflections in the cab window. Mick looked cool and fresh, her wavy, dark brown hair and dark skin glistening in the sun. I, on the other hand, looked like a pale, limp, blond dishrag.

Mick's mom and dad came out to greet us. "Welcome to Australia!" Mrs. Kennard said. "We're so happy to have you for the summer. I hope Mick hasn't tired you out already with her plans."

"Well," I said, smiling. "I'm a little confused right now. It's hard to get used to the fact that it's summer here and winter back home. But I'm sure I'll—"

"—feel better after a nap and a good meal," Mr. Kennard said. "You must be exhausted after your long trip. Mick, grab the suitcases and take them to your room. Come inside, Dusty."

They led me into the house, through the big, open kitchen and into the comfortable living room. I sank into the soft cushions on the couch and took the cold drink that Mrs. Kennard handed me. As soon as I finished my drink, she bustled me off to the room that I was going to share with Mick, and she tucked me into bed.

"Sleep, Dusty," she said.

My eyes shut almost immediately. But for a few minutes my mind danced on. It was nice to be taken care of. Mick's parents seemed really nice. I promised myself that, when I woke up and felt better, I really had to give Mick another chance. After all, I probably

18

seemed just as strange to her.

Several hours later, I opened my eyes to get the shock of my life. Two inches away from my face, a pair of brown eyes were staring back at me!

"Aaarrgh!" I yelled, leaping off the bed.

"Sorry, mate," Mick said, doubling over in laughter. "I was just taking a look, that's all."

"A look at what?"

"Your eyelashes," she said. "I've never seen anyone with such long eyelashes. Are they false?"

I folded my arms over my chest. "No!"

"Do you put mascara on them?"

I rolled my eyes.

"Sorry. They just look unnatural, that's all. Mine are so short, you can't even see them. It's a family trait. See!"

She stuck her face in front of mine and blinked her eyes.

Her eyelashes *were* short. "Uhh, I've heard you can buy some kind of cream to put on them to make them grow."

"Really?"

"I don't know much about that sort of thing. Most of the other girls in my school are wearing makeup. But I have more important things to do," I said, sitting back down on the bed.

"Like what?"

"Well, like flying," I said. "I'm pretty close to getting my pilot's license. "All I have left are my fifteen solo hours. I've already passed the ground school requirements and all of my dual flight time with an instructor." I didn't mention that I had to wait until I was sixteen to solo and until I was seventeen to get my actual license.

"Wow," Mick said. "Maybe your dreaming would be a bird if you were an aborigine."

Yuck, I thought. *Just when I thought we were going to have a normal conversation!*

I sighed as I got up to put away some of my things. I laid my jeans and T-shirts in one drawer and my underwear and socks in another. Mick sat on the chair, watching me. I wondered if she was waiting for me to ask her some questions about Australia. *Well,* I told myself, *it would be better than talking about my family and the mess I had left behind.*

I paused as I was folding my shirts. "So, Mick," I said. "Why don't you tell me more about that dreamtime stuff and about how you became a humanoid red ant?"

She looked down. "I didn't know if you were interested," she said.

"Well, you have to admit it's kind of a weird idea. Do you believe it, or is it just a kind of superstition, like black cats and not walking under ladders?"

Mick didn't answer for a while. I was about to repeat the question when she said, "I don't know if I believe it or not, Dusty. It all seems kind of weird, like you say. Here in the city everything is modern and new, with cars and television and computers. But out in the country, far away from everything modern—I don't know."

I was beginning to get a little bit interested. "Well, how did you hear about these legends?"

Mick sat down on the floor as the sun began to sink outside her bedroom window. "My grandfather lived in the bush, the outback, in the old-fashioned way of my people," Mick explained. "When I visited him, he would tell me lots of stories. I guess I sort of grew up believing them. It's different in the outback. Things are..."

"Things are what?"

But she didn't answer, but said instead, "I'll tell you a story he told me, and you can decide for yourself."

I nodded.

"A long time ago," Mick began, "there was nothing on the earth. No trees, no water, no plants, no animals."

"No people," I added.

"Right," Mick said. "And then our spirit ancestors decided to come up out of the earth's crust and sing it into being. Each one traveled far and wide, singing."

"Singing what?"

"They sang secret songs that created all the rivers, every lake, every rock, every leaf and branch. They sang every *soak*, waterhole, hill, plain, and *clay pan*. And each one taught these secret songlines to his children, and they taught their children. Each aborigine knows a portion of his songline, and it hooks up with everyone else's songline. And aborigines believe that we have to keep singing them, or else..."

"Or else what?"

"Or else the world will disappear," Mick whispered.

I laughed uncomfortably. "So you're telling me that a bunch of people in Australia think they're related to ants, or butterflies, or whatever, and have to sing these secret songs to hold the world together?"

Mick just shrugged. "That's the story my grandfather told me."

"Wait a minute," I said. "This is just a tall tale that you tell to all the Americans who come here, isn't it? You're pulling my leg."

But again, she didn't answer. I was getting

a little worried that she might really believe the story.

"My grandfather said that our songline follows the path of the unfailing waterholes in the outback."

"Water's pretty important in the outback, isn't it?"

Mick nodded. But she had a weird, serious look on her face. "Here's another story he told me. It's a legend of the red ant people."

I waited.

"Long ago," she began, "my red ant brothers and sisters dreamed and sang fairly near here in the desert beyond the mountains. They built these gigantic ant hills filled with many connecting labyrinths—you know, mazes. My ancestors were much larger than the red ants you almost stepped on today. They were bigger, even, than people."

"Red ants, bigger than people," I muttered.

Mick went on in spite of me. "My grandfather told me that the ant labyrinths were lined with precious opals. He said that he had seen them, and so have others in our clan. He told me of a beautiful grotto that shines with an unearthly light of its own because of the reflection of millions of opals."

"Really?"

"According to our customs, when you reach

a certain age, you take part in a song ritual where everyone of your clan sings his own *tjuringa,* or piece of the songline. Then, at the end of the song, you find and enter the lost labyrinths."

"And grab your share of the opals?" I asked, grinning.

Mick shook her head. "No way. The treasure inside the hills *is* worth a fortune. But no red ant clan member would ever steal it."

"Someone else might, though," I pointed out. "Aren't other people looking for these labyrinths with the fortune in opals?"

"Sure they are. People have been trying to find the hills for centuries. But no one has."

"But what if someone does find them?" I said.

"The legend says that only those of the red ant clan can enter the labyrinth and return alive. It's not only opals that are in there, you know. There are also billions of red ants, red ants that could make really short work of an intruder—if you know what I mean."

I knew what she meant. And even though it was still hot, I shuddered at the thought of billions of red ants slowly eating a person alive!

Mick went on. "No prospector out to find the opals has ever come back. They've all disappeared without a trace in the outback."

"Hold on! That doesn't prove anything. I've seen the Crocodile Dundee movies. The outback's a wilderness, and I bet people get lost out there all the time."

"I'll tell you one more story, then," Mick said. "About 40 years ago, right after the war, there was a prospector named Wild Joe. He had lived in Adelaide since he was born. A real dinkum—that means true—Aussie! His parents had lived here since they were born. His great-great-great-grandfather was brought over here on a prisoner ship from England.

"Anyway, I guess you could say he knew the land as well as anyone. Sometimes he would disappear for months at a time with only a knife and a flint in his *swag*. Everyone would think he was dead. But then he would turn up, safe and sound, with a pocketful of opals or gold, enough to live on for a year or more. And he always wore a huge golden ring with an magnificent opal set in it."

"Then he would go out again?" I asked.

Mick leaned forward. "Yes," she whispered. "He would go out again. And every time, he would tell his buddies at the claims office that he was getting close to the big one—the red ant dreaming site—the opal labyrinths.

He said he was singing his way there, just like the aborigines, one track at a time."

"But how did he find out about the aborigine songlines?"

"Nobody knows. Like I said, he knew the land as well as anyone. He had his sources. Some aborigines trusted him. So maybe they told him. Anyway, the last time he was in town, he went to the claims office and told them he had found out the tune to the last part of the songline. They lent him money for mules to carry back the opals, and he went off into the outback."

"Let me guess," I said. "He was never heard from again?"

"Not exactly," Mick said in a low voice, looking around as if she didn't want anyone to hear her. "Two weeks later, the mules wandered back into Adelaide. They had gone insane from whatever it was they had seen. They were foaming at the mouth and blind and had to be shot."

"Wasn't Wild Joe with them?"

Mick paused. "Part of him was," she said softly.

I gulped as goose bumps popped out all over my arms.

"Part?" I whispered.

"Just his hand," she told me, "with his gold

ring on the finger. They found it in one of the saddlebags. And in his hand were two of the most perfect opals anyone had ever seen."

She stared at me with wide eyes. I stared right back. Then I grinned and said, "That was a good one, Mick. You really had me going there for a minute. Remind me to tell you the story of the one-armed brakeman."

"It's not just a story," Mick said. "Tomorrow we'll go to the city museum. You can see the perfect opals there, along with the gold ring they cut off of Wild Joe's mangled hand."

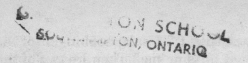
CHAPTER THREE
The Initiation

I spent the next few days recovering from the jet lag I told Mick I didn't have. That and being depressed about the big change coming up at home. Mick and I did a few tourist things, including seeing Wild Joe's ring at the city museum. But my heart wasn't in it. I tried to be interested in Australia. But I just couldn't help thinking about Mom and Dad and how they could have done something like this to me. I thought everything was perfect the way it was. And now things were going to be changed forever.

One morning, I woke up from a dream about the horrors of having a baby in the house. Already, it was hot enough to make me sweat. I rolled over on the sticky sheets and burst out crying. Mick was beside me in a second.

"Miss your folks?" she asked.

"Why should I?" I said, sobbing. "I'll bet they're not missing me." Then I just blurted out the whole story about Mom and Dad having the baby.

Mick listened quietly. Then she said, "I don't think having a brother would be that bad."

I groaned.

"I used to have a brother," she said. "He was killed in a car crash when he was six."

I looked at her through my tears. "Oh, I'm so sorry, Mick—"

"That's all right," she said.

I decided right then and there that I had better shape up. It was disgusting. I mean, there I was in a great new country, and all I could do was feel sorry for myself!

"I'm really sorry. You must think I'm the worst guest in the world," I said. "All I do is whine."

Mick ignored my apology and started talking about our plans for the day. "We're going to a wallaby race, and on a tour of the city. There's going to be a carnival with sheep-shearing contests and an outback triathlon. Then we're going to eat some *yabbies* and *floaters*—that's a meat pie floating upside down in pea soup with a dab of tomato sauce on top, and then—"

"Whoa!" I cried. "Slow down. Maybe we'd better do one thing at a time, huh?"

We spent that day and the next looking around Adelaide. We did see some interesting things. Adelaide actually started out as a kind of Australian Wild West town, with prospectors and ranchers and farmers. But even though I tried as hard as I could, I couldn't help wondering how things were going at home. Were Mom and Dad looking through baby name books? Were they picking out a stroller? Were they painting my computer room baby blue?

As we walked home at the end of a long day, I saw an airplane flying over. I squinted into the sun and explained to Mick, "That's a Lockheed L-1011. They're really neat. They can practically fly themselves, they're so advanced."

"You really like flying, don't you, mate?"

"More than just about anything."

Mick looked at me but didn't say anything.

I didn't think anything more about it until dinner the next day. I noticed that Mick's parents seemed unusually happy, and Mick looked kind of like the cat that ate the canary.

"Go ahead and tell her," Mr. Kennard said to Mick. He nodded at me.

Mick looked at her fingernails and said casually, "Umm, remember how you said the other day that you liked flying?"

"Uhh, sure I remember."

"Well, do you think you might want to go on an airplane trip?"

"What?" I said, wanting to make sure I heard correctly. "That would be fantastic!"

Mick and her parents laughed and told me the plan. They had all noticed that I didn't seem too happy there, and they looked around for something I might like to do. Mick told them about how I was taking flying lessons, and Mr. Kennard got an idea.

"There's this air tour of Flinders Ranges National Park and a view of opal mining in a place called Coober Pedy," Mick said. "My dad checked and the student exchange organization will pay for one special trip. So, it's all set. We leave tomorrow!"

I squealed with joy, got up and hugged the whole family. Then I sat down again, but I was too excited to finish my dinner, and so I got up and hugged them all again!

Mick and I stayed up pretty late that night packing for the trip. I think we were both too excited to sleep because we kept talking even after we turned out the light. But the funny thing was, what we were saying had nothing to do with each other.

"I wonder if the pilot will let me go up to the cockpit and look around?" I said.

Then Mick said, "Maybe Wild Joe is still wandering around out in the desert somewhere, looking for his missing hand and his gold ring!"

"Tomorrow morning, I'll get a map and plot out our route, just as if I were going to fly it. That way, we'll know where we're going!"

"Wouldn't it be great if we accidentally spotted the opal labyrinths from the air?" Mick said. "Hey, wait a minute." Her voice sounded serious.

"What is it?" I asked.

"I just thought of something. If we do see the red ant labyrinths," she said, "it could be trouble because you're not initiated into the clan, into our tribe."

"I don't get it."

"I've been initiated, but you haven't," Mick explained. "The girls and women in our clan have a special ceremony. It's for becoming a teenager, and for welcoming a new woman into the tribe."

"That's nice," I mumbled, beginning to feel sleepy.

"Come on," Mick cried, shaking me. "Get out of bed."

"Why?" I said. "I'm tired."

"We're going to do the ceremony," she said. "It'll make us like sisters, and it'll make you one of us, the red ant people."

I still couldn't tell if she took it all seriously. But I knew I wasn't going to get out of it. I got out of bed and sat on the floor. Mick didn't turn on the light. In the dark, I could see her cross the room to her desk and open a drawer. She brought a basket of stuff back to where I was sitting. Then from against her wall, she carried over a flat, round stone, put it on the floor between us like a table and sat down.

Then she started doing something pretty strange. While singing a song in a language I didn't understand, she took things out of the basket. They looked like lumps of clay or rock. She placed them carefully on the stone. She lit a match and touched it to the top of one lump. It caught and glowed red, casting an eerie light onto Mick's face.

Then, whatever she lit gave off a smell. It didn't smell bad. But, I couldn't explain exactly what it smelled like. Maybe it was some kind of incense or scented candle. It reminded me of being outdoors, of camping, of nature. Mick placed a hat of sticks, string, and feathers on my head. I sat there, balancing it,

33

wondering what in the world she would do next.

She began to chant, raising her hands to the ceiling. It was pretty weird. I had never seen anyone in a trance before. Maybe I was kind of in a trance, too, because I imagined the room slipping away from us. It almost felt as if we had been transported to the outback, the home of her people.

I watched, spellbound, as Mick took one of the other lumps and drew lines on her face and arms. Then, she reached over and drew matching lines on my face and arms. All the while, she sang softly. Sometimes her voice was soft, sometimes hard, sometimes melodious and sometimes harsh. I guessed she was singing songs about the legends of her clan.

Then suddenly, I noticed that the tune had changed. She sang a line in her aborigine language and then paused, as if she were waiting for someone to repeat the line.

I realized that someone was me.

Mick sang the line again, touched my hand, and then waited with her eyes closed.

Oh well, I decided. *I might as well sing along. It's kind of like being at summer camp.*

I didn't know what I was saying, but I repeated each line that Mick sang. I thought about how my friends at home would freak out if they saw me doing this. But somehow, it didn't seem so out of place here, not with Mick, not with our trip into the outback coming up the next day. I felt as if this meant a lot to her, for us to become like sisters, for me to be initiated into her clan.

She drew pictures on the stone, concentric circles and a series of lines. I drew matching pictures. She sang. I sang.

And the smoky scent of the outback swirled around us, coming closer and closer.

CHAPTER FOUR
Wings Over Australia

EARLY the next day, the Kennards dropped us off at the airport to catch a small plane for the tour of Flinders Ranges National Park. Mr. Kennard told me the mountain range started outside of Adelaide and ran 120 miles inland until it disappeared into the desert. He also said that most of the houses in the small outback town of Coober Pedy were underground because it's so hot out there. Even their church was built underground.

I thanked the Kennards about a million times for letting us go on this trip. "Have a great time," Mick's dad said as we headed for the plane. "Got your map, Dusty?"

"Sure do." He had given me a map at breakfast, and I had plotted out where we were going. We waved goodbye.

"In Aborigine, *Coober Pedy* means 'man in hole,'" Mick told me as we boarded the airplane. "Good name, huh?"

"Yeah," I answered. I was busy checking out the plane. The curtain was drawn back. So I peeked into the cockpit. The pilot and the copilot were already in there, flipping switches and calling in a check to the tower.

They looked up and smiled. "Hello girls," the copilot said.

"Hi," I said. "My name is Dusty Martin, and this is my friend, Mick. I'm visiting with her family for the summer. I'm a student pilot, you know."

The pilot reached back to shake our hands. "It's always good to have a backup pilot on board," he said, nodding at his copilot, who also shook our hands. "Come on up later for a visit. I'm Skip, and this is Doyle."

"Thanks. We'd like that," I told him.

"I've never seen the cockpit of an airplane before," Mick said when we were settled in our seats. "It sure is small, and there are an awful lot of buttons."

"It's easy once you have a little practice," I said. "The panel seemed complicated to me, too, at first. But you learn what each button and dial is for."

As I sat back in my seat, I couldn't help

imagining that this plane was taking me home. Sure, I was beginning to like Australia. But I was still homesick. I knew I wasn't going to be able to take a plane ride every day to keep my mind off my troubles.

I closed my eyes and imagined my computer room back home. I could see my desk, made out of a door propped up on top of two file cabinets. I saw my shelves of books and my flight simulator computer game. Then suddenly, the image blurred and a crib replaced the desk. I heard a baby crying.

I opened my eyes. Sitting right across the aisle was a woman with a crying baby. Her husband sat in front of her and was turning around, making disgusting goo-goo noises.

"Sh, sh, sh. Hush now," the mother said. "Mama will sing you a little song, and then you can go to sleep on the pretty airplane."

I almost gagged. *Why do they let passengers bring babies on tours like this?* The mother began singing.

I turned my head away and tried to concentrate on the other passengers as they boarded. There were two aboriginal men, and a woman who seemed familiar. Then I noticed her battered duffel bag. It was Nancy, the American woman who had sat next to me on the plane from Sydney.

"Hey, Dusty," she said. "Are you enjoying Australia yet?"

"It's getting there," I told her.

She chuckled. "As long as you're off of the ground, huh?"

I grinned and nodded.

I was about to introduce her to Mick, but just then, the pilot announced that we would be taking off as soon as everyone had fastened their seatbelts.

Nancy moved on and sat in the back row. "She's the woman who sat next to me on the flight into Adelaide," I whispered to Mick. "I'll introduce you."

I turned around to Nancy, but she was busy looking for something in her bag. Instead, the mother next to me said hello.

"Hi," I said.

"Hi," Mick said. "You sure have a cute baby."

I groaned inwardly.

"How old is he?" Mick asked, with me in the middle.

"He's six months old," she told her. "His name is Anthony." She couldn't resist snuggling Anthony's chin as she said that.

I was ready to throw up. I was trying to tell Mick with eye signals to stop paying attention to the baby. But Mick wouldn't stop. By the time the plane had taxied from the terminal onto the runway, Mick had introduced us (their last name was Fernandez), had explained why I was in Australia, and had found out that they were both school teachers from Melbourne on vacation.

"He's soooo cute," Mick cooed.

I knew any second Mick would ask to hold the little creature, and I'd have to reach for the air sickness bag!

"Do you think I could hold him?" Mick asked.

"Certainly. I'm sure Anthony would like that. Wouldn't you?" Mrs. Fernandez asked, her voice high-pitched and squeaky. The baby giggled, gurgled and made generally obnoxious sounds.

"We're taking off!" I finally cried, exasperated by all of the baby talk. Everyone paid attention to themselves during the takeoff, but a moment later, Mick leaned across me again, ready to start up another baby conversation and to get her chance to hold darling Anthony.

"Look!" I said loudly, leaning in front of Mick to point out of the window. "We're heading out over the ocean."

As I hoped, that got Mick's attention. "Why?" she asked, pressing her face against the glass. "Coober Pedy is inland."

It worked. I was glad to have her mind off Anthony for a minute.

"It's the wind," I answered. "You have to take off into the wind. Then the pilot will bank and head inland for the tour."

Sure enough, a few minutes later, Skip turned the plane and headed up the coast. Mick pointed out St. Vincent Gulf, the Yorke Peninsula, and Spencer Gulf. About an hour into our trip, we crossed over Eyre Peninsula and the little town of Port Lincoln right out on the point. Skip followed the Flinders Highway along the coast for another hour, and then turned inland just before Streaky Bay. It was all on my map. I showed Mick the route I had plotted.

"In less than an hour, we should be crossing the Trans-Australian Railway," I said.

We gazed down at the barren countryside. I was glad that this was a six-hour trip. After a while, the coastal view flattened out into an endless desert. We both strained to see out of the tiny window. "Do you see any tracks yet?" Mick asked.

"Not yet, but the desert is beginning to show up on the left. Boy, I wouldn't want to be stuck out there without a water bottle," I said, looking out over the huge expanse of the Great Victoria Desert.

41

"Speaking of water. How about if we break out the lunch bags. It's noon," she announced, picking up my wrist and turning my watch in her direction.

"Sounds good to me. This is a no-frills tour," I joked. All around us the other passengers were digging into their bags to eat lunch.

"You didn't ask for luxury," Mick said, laughing. "Just a chance to fly."

"I know, and it's great," I said, looking at Mick and smiling.

"It's hard to believe my grandfather used to live out there with his people," Mick told me as she munched on her fish sandwich.

"It's hard to believe anyone could survive out there," I said.

"When I was little, he used to take me on day trips to the desert and show me how to dig for grubs and stuff. We stayed in his *humpy*—his shack—and every day we'd boil up a *billy* for tea—that's just a pot of tea—eat *damper* bread, and hunt for *kampararpa*."

"For what?"

"*Kampararpa* is a kind of tiny wild tomato."

"Oh."

"It's good *bush tucker*. That means good outback food."

"This sandwich is good *bush tucker*, too."

"Look! There they are!" Mick practically

shouted. "The tracks. And look, in the distance, I think I see Coober Pedy."

"Or else a mirage," I replied. "According to my map, Coober Pedy has to be at least another 170 miles."

"How long will that take?" Mrs. Fernandez asked. "I want to take lots of pictures."

"Planes like this usually fly about 200 miles an hour. So, it should only take about 45 more minutes."

While Mrs. Fernandez handed Anthony to her husband and rummaged in her camera case, I leaned toward the window and tried to locate landmarks. It seemed as if we should have been flying fairly close to the Stuart Highway. But I didn't see a road below us or on either side of the plane.

Forty-five minutes came and went, and the town that Mick saw in the distance turned out to be a ridge of eucalyptus and desert oak. The gray-green leaves reflected the afternoon sun and contrasted with the red dirt below.

Another ten minutes passed, then twenty, then thirty.

"I think we're off course," I whispered to Mick.

"I doubt it," Mick said cheerfully. "These guys probably have been flying this tour for years. I don't think they could get lost."

I lowered my voice a little more. "I didn't say they were lost. I said they were off course." I pointed to the map.

"Maybe they're making another turn so that we can see Coober Pedy from a better angle."

"We should have flown over Coober Pedy half an hour ago," I said.

"Well, maybe this plane doesn't fly as fast as you think it does," Mick suggested.

"There's no highway beneath us," I pointed out to Mick.

"They're taking us on the scenic route?" Mick asked hopefully. But I could see she was starting to look concerned.

We both looked out the window.

"I think we're in trouble," I said. "What does that big white thing we're flying over look like to you?"

"Lake Eyre?"

I pointed to the huge space on my map where the usually dry reservoir covered thousands of square miles. "Look at the sun. We're flying northeast. Away from Coober Pedy. And away from Flinders Ranges as well."

Mick and I looked at each other.

"We haven't heard the pilots announce any scenery for at least an hour," I whispered.

"Do you think something's wrong, mate?" Mick whispered back.

"I think," I said quietly so that the other passengers wouldn't hear, "I think we'd better go check with the crew."

Slowly Mick and I got up and walked the few feet toward the curtain that screened the pilots from the passengers. Just as I reached out to open the curtain, the plane lurched wildly to the left and then to the right.

All the passengers ended up in the aisle.

Mick and I heard screaming as we were thrown through the curtain into the cockpit!

"Aarrgghh!" I groaned as I fell between the seats. My shoulder hit the stick. My forehead rammed into the instrument panel. Stunned for a few seconds, I tried to push myself free. But there was a soft, heavy weight on top of me. Mick must have tumbled against me when we fell.

"Mick! Mick! Are you all right?" I shouted, pushing against her. But I couldn't budge her.

"I'm fine," she groaned from the other side of the cockpit. "What's going on?"

That's when I realized that the person on top of me wasn't Mick. Wincing at the pain, I reached over my shoulder. My fingers felt the bald head of Skip, the pilot.

Don't panic, I told myself. It was no use. "Mick! Help!" I screamed. "Get him off of me!"

That's when I heard it. Even with all the scrambling in the passenger compartment, I heard the change in the sound of the engines. They were sputtering. I looked over for the first time toward the copilot's seat. He, too, was slumped over in his harness.

I twisted my head up, struggling to see the instrument panel.

"Oh, no!" I cried in shock and fear. The low fuel light was blinking. And next to it, the automatic pilot indicator light flickered once...twice...and went out.

The plane immediately took a dive.

"PULL!" I yelled. "Pull him off me or we're all going to die!"

With all her strength, Mick dragged the unconscious pilot off of me. I jumped into his seat and grabbed the stick, pulling back with all of my might. Sweat broke out on my forehead. I took great gasps of air as I watched the desert rising fast to meet the nose of the falling plane.

"Please!" I screamed. "Please let there be enough fuel to pull us out of this dive!"

I stared as the ground came closer and closer. Everything seemed to be in slow motion. I saw myself at the stick, trying to remember all of the emergency safety measures my instructor had taught me.

But first, the plane started to spin. I focused on a central point to avoid getting dizzy and gave the plane right rudder to neutralize the spin. Slowly, miraculously, the plane stopped its wild, uncontrolled spinning. But we were still heading straight down.

My arms strained as I pulled back the stick. Sweat stung my eyes. My stomach was in my throat, and my throat was stuck somewhere on the back of my neck.

If only I had enough time—and also enough fuel.

I could make out the individual branches of bushes and the silvery glow of the gum trees as the ground came ever closer. The roar of the wind and the screams of the passengers filled my ears. I closed my eyes, thinking I would never open them again.

CHAPTER FIVE
You Look Like You've Seen A Ghost!

WHEN I opened my eyes a second later, I saw blue sky.

"Are we in heaven?" I whispered.

Mick leaped over the limp pilot and clapped me on the back. "You did it!" she yelled. "You did it! I can't believe it. You saved us!"

"I—I did?" It took me a whole three seconds to realize I still had a death grip on the stick and that the plane was heading almost straight up in the air. I eased forward on the stick and leveled the plane out. Looking out the window, I realized how close we had come to crashing. I tried to put it out of my mind.

I smiled at Mick. "I guess I did, didn't I?"

"Wow! That was great, unbelievable! I've never seen anyone fly like that! You didn't tell me you were a stunt pilot!"

"I'm not," I said. "I was just trying to save

us!" I felt my heart finally beginning to slow down to normal. "Are they dead?" I asked, nodding at Skip and Doyle.

Mick placed two fingers against each of their necks. "No," she said. "I can feel their pulses. And they're both breathing. I wonder what happened."

"What happened is that we're completely off course and almost out of fuel," I said, wondering how long the fuel light had been blinking.

"They must have been unconscious for a long time," Mick said.

"I don't know," I replied. "But I have to turn this plane around right away. Go tell the others what happened. See if everyone is all right. I'm going to radio for help."

Mick went into the cabin, and I picked up the radio microphone. Pushing the button to *send,* I started calling in. "Adelaide airport? This is Opal Tours charter flight number 147. We're in trouble. Request assistance."

I waited for the answering static, but there was none. In fact, there was nothing. Not even a click. I pushed the *send* button several more times. Nothing but silence.

"Maybe the cord's tangled," I muttered. Reaching down, I tugged slightly on the black wire. It came loose in my hand. The neatly

49

sliced end told me everything that I needed to know.

"Sabotage," I whispered to Mick when she came back to the cockpit a few minutes later. I showed her the cut cord.

"But who could have done it?"

"I don't know. But whoever did it wanted us all to die!"

"Hurry up," Mick said frantically, with real fear in her voice. "Get us back home."

"Mick, I've turned the plane around, but we don't have enough fuel to get back."

Just then the right engine sputtered to a halt. Mick's eyes were round with fright as she stared at me. Before I could say a word, we heard the other engine burp and then go silent.

"Hold on," I said gripping the controls more firmly. "We're going down."

I knew all those hours of practicing glide landings were paying off. My instructor had said that you never know when you're going to need that skill. I had practiced over and over until I could land the little plane any-where—on the runway, in a field, on a road.

But I had never had to land in the sand be-tween trees and bushes. And rocks. There were so many rocks.

I searched the ground for a long, flat area,

while Mick gripped the back of the copilot's seat next to me.

"Lower the landing gear," I said. "It's that white knob on the right."

Mick reached for the landing gear switch. I sighed with relief when I heard the sound of the wheels coming out from the belly of the plane. In front of me I saw a stand of gum trees on top of a rocky ridge. Beyond that was a stretch of red, sandy dirt with only a few small bushes.

"I'm heading for that spot," I said pointing.

"You'll never make it," she said. "You'll hit the trees."

"There's nowhere else," I said. "I don't have any choice. I have to try."

Mick held her breath as we approached the ridge. So did I. We were coming in awfully low—too low. I held on to the stick.

"Steady. Steady," I mumbled to myself. "Hold it."

At the last minute, I felt sure we were going to skim the top branches and flip over. But suddenly, a little rise of warm air in front of the ridge lifted us clear. I set the plane down as gently as I could on the rough ground. We bumped to a stop at the edge of a deep ravine.

I looked out the window over the edge. It

dropped off about 30 feet into a rock-filled canyon. All I could do was stare. If we had rolled a few feet farther, it could have been bad, very bad.

I slowly let all the air out of my lungs and slumped back in my seat. "Is everyone all right?" I called back into the cabin.

For one long moment, they all stared at me, in what I guess was probably shock. Then, all together, they burst into applause.

Mr. Fernandez spoke for all of them. "We're just glad to be alive!" he said.

"You said it!" one of the aborigine men added.

Then everyone was yelling at once. I guess I had been so busy trying to fly the plane that I didn't realize how terrified everyone was. We all just sat there trying to absorb the fact that we were all alive. We had made it!

Then reality hit. We were out in the middle of nowhere—no fuel, no water, no food (except what we had all brought for our own lunches), no radio, and no way of getting home.

"Does anyone know any first aid?" I asked. "The pilots are out cold."

"I'll take a look," Mrs. Fernandez said, handing the baby to her husband.

Things moved pretty quickly after that. Everyone helped each other gather their things and get off of the plane. The men lifted Skip and Doyle and carried them into the shade underneath a wing of the plane. Mrs. Fernandez, it turned out, had helped out her school's nurse. It wasn't like having a doctor there, but it was all we had.

She checked the pilots over and looked up into the faces of the other passengers.

"I think they were drugged," she said.

"Are you sure?" Mr. Fernandez asked.

"I think so," she said. "Their pulse is slow, and their breathing is deep—the same symptoms as someone who's been anesthetized for an operation."

"But who could have done such a thing?" Mick asked. "Didn't they know that the plane would run out of fuel and crash? We all would have been—killed."

We all looked suspiciously at each other.

"Maybe it was hijackers," said the first aborigine man, who said his name was Gil.

"Smugglers?" his friend John suggested.

Everyone began talking at once.

"Maybe there's something very valuable on the plane that someone wants," said Mr. Fernandez.

"Or maybe the pilots had enemies, and someone wanted them dead—even if it meant killing all of us," Mrs. Fernandez added.

"But why?" asked Nancy. "I mean. This is just a sightseeing trip. These are ordinary people—pilots who've been working for this company for years. What kind of enemies could they possibly have?"

"I don't know," Gil said. "Someone drugged them, though. They sure didn't drug themselves. And whoever did it might be right here among us."

"Or out there," Nancy said, sweeping her arm, "waiting to gun us down like rabbits."

We all stood around hoping an answer would pop out of the air. But, of course, it didn't. We were all afraid of what we didn't know. And nobody knew whom to trust.

"I guess we'll just have to wait until the pilots come to," Mrs. Fernandez said. "Maybe we'll have our answers then."

"In the meantime, we're stuck out here, hundreds of miles from the nearest town," John said. "How are we going to get back?"

While the adults argued about the best thing to do, Mick and I wandered away from the group.

"I think we should go back into the plane and check around for clues," Mick whispered.

"Yeah. Maybe it was just an accident, and they both got sick at the same time. Food poisoning," I said. "That could be it."

"Or maybe it wasn't an accident, and we'll find something important that will point to who did it."

As casually as we could, we climbed back into the plane. "You take the cabin. I'll take the cockpit," I said.

Mick lifted seat cushions and checked in the storage compartments. I crawled around in the cockpit, but I didn't see anything except the normal stuff someone would expect to find after a trip—soda cans, papers, assorted junk. Under the pilot's seat, I found a thermos with some coffee still in it. There was a coffee stain in the lid cup and some in a cup stuck in the holder next to the copilot's seat.

"They drank coffee," I muttered. "Maybe the drug was in the coffee."

I set the thermos near the curtain and kept looking. There was nothing unusual on the instrument panel, on the seats, or in the pockets of their jackets. The last place I had to look was in a sliding drawer, kind of like a glove compartment in a car, right beneath the little closet where passengers could hang their coats. A shiver of fear struck me as I reached for the release latch. What if there was a mangled hand in there, clutching some opals, like Wild Joe's?

"Get a hold of yourself, Dusty," I said aloud. "That's silly."

"What's silly?" Mick asked, coming through the curtain.

"Oh, nothing," I said, releasing the latch and pulling the door open. "I was just letting my imagination run wild. Did you find anything out there?"

"Not a thing."

"Well, this is the last place I have to look."

The drawer slid open smoothly. Inside was a bundle of cloth.

"What's that?" Mick asked.

"Beats me," I said, lifting the cloth out. "There's something inside it—something hard."

Slowly, I peeled off the cloth, which was old and musty. There were strange symbols carved on it. "Mick, have you ever seen anything like this? Is this some kind of writing?"

But she didn't answer. She was staring at the bundle with wide eyes. Finally I had the thing unwrapped and held it up for Mick.

Mick gasped.

"What? What is it?" I asked, turning the oval-shaped piece of carved wood over in my hands.

"It's a—it's a—*tjuringa*," Mick whispered.

"Huh? You mean one of those things that's

a piece of a songline, like you were telling me about?"

She nodded, studying the wood.

"What do all of these symbols mean?" There was a large spiral in the center, surrounded by smaller spirals. Lines connected the circles and led off the edges of the wood.

Mick took a step backward. Her hands shook as she brought them up to cover her mouth.

"Mick! Does this have something to do with your ancestors?" I demanded. "Mick! Say something! You look like you've seen a ghost!"

Then she mumbled a word in Aborigine, a word that gave me a shiver of fear. It was a word I had recognized from our ceremony of the night before.

It was the aborigine name for red ant.

CHAPTER SIX
Flames In The Desert

"GET a grip, Mick!" I hissed, pressing the object into her trembling hands. "This is just a piece of old wood!"

But Mick wasn't listening. She stared off into space, muttering to herself words I couldn't understand. I waved my hand in front of her face. No response.

"The *tjuringa* is the sacred board," she mumbled, her voice far away and spooky. I could tell she didn't know I was there. Then she said something that really scared me.

"Yes, Grandfather," she said in a ghostly voice. "I remember. The ants came out of the ground in Lake Eyre. They flew into the air and came down as men. They burrowed deep into the bowl caused by the falling sun and created the opals. Follow the line of unfailing waterholes to the ridge above the lake that no longer is."

The look on Mick's face scared the daylights out of me. It was as if she wasn't in the plane at all. She was back in time with her grandfather, under this same wide desert sky.

"The ants, now men, built their labyrinth city to hide the sun they had captured in the opals," she went on, paying no attention to me. I didn't know whether to try to wake her up or just let her go on. I was afraid something terrible might happen if I tried to snap her out of her trance.

Suddenly her voice changed. It was low, and her eyebrows were drawn together in the center, her mouth turned down. She sounded like an old man talking.

"Our people's law says that no uninitiated person may gaze on the *tjuringa*. It is the soul of the owner of the dreaming track. Those who walk with heavy feet on the pure soul of another will pay with their lives."

This was too much. She seemed to be taken over by—something. A shiver ran down my spine.

"Mick!" I said, shaking her shoulders. "Stop it! Get a hold of yourself! Snap out of it!"

Mick shook her head, and her eyes focused on my face. For a long time, she stared into my eyes as if she didn't recognize me. There was a strange light in her eyes that looked almost like flames. I figured it must have been the sun reflecting off something in the cockpit.

Suddenly, she dropped the *tjuringa* and gripped my shoulders. "Dusty! I saw flames!"

My mouth dropped open. Had I also seen fire reflected in her eyes? No way! It had to be a reflection of the bright desert sun.

"Are you all right, Mick? I thought you were gone for a moment."

"Dusty, I was gone. It was so weird. I was a little kid again. Grandfather and I were sitting at his campfire and he was telling me the story of the red ant labyrinths. We stood up and he pointed toward a rock outcropping away in the distance. He told me to search for my destiny behind the stone wall dreaming site. And he warned me about uninitiated people looking at the *tjuringa*."

"I know," I said softly. "I heard him."

Mick stared at me for another second, then said, "We should leave it where we found it. The *tjuringa* is powerful. It's dangerous."

"I know," I said. "But this could be why the pilots were drugged. We have to keep it from falling into the wrong hands."

I picked up the *tjuringa* and wrapped the cloth back around it. I put it in my backpack.

"You're right," Mick said. "If someone who's not a red ant tries to sing the *tjuringa* without the rest of the cycle, then…"

Once again Mick grew silent.

"But Mick, what would happen if someone sang the *tjuringa* out of sequence?"

"Remember that I told you that the aborigines believe that the world was sung into being?"

"Uh-huh. And that you have song-cycle ceremonies to keep it in existence."

"Well, not singing the song would be terrible," Mick said. "But singing it out of order would be worse."

"What do you mean by worse?"

She touched my bag where the *tjuringa* made a slight bulge. "Aborigines believe that singing the songline out of order would destroy the world."

"Wait a minute!" I cried. "That can't be true. Do you really believe that?"

Mick looked at me with her dark, brown eyes, eyes that reminded me of the vast desert around us. "I don't know what I believe, Dusty. But after what I just experienced when I touched the *tjuringa,* can we afford to take the chance?"

This was *too* strange. But somehow I felt that she was right. We just had to protect the *tjuringa*.

"Do you think this *tjuringa* is the key?" I asked. "Like maybe whoever smuggled it on board was looking for those labyrinths you were talking about?"

"Just like Wild Joe," she whispered. "He had a *tjuringa,* too, the missing link, he bragged to everyone, that completed the songline and would lead him to the opals."

"What happened to the one he had?" I asked.

"It was never found. I wonder," she said. "Could this be...?"

"I don't know. But we've got to keep this a secret," I said, patting my bag. "This *tjuringa* might be something people are willing to kill for. And if it is the cause of the sabotage, then the person who drugged the pilots could be watching us right now."

"We have to watch to see what they all do when we come out of the plane empty-handed," Mick said. "I know. Let's take this thermos to them. It'll keep them busy so that they won't think we found anything else."

We were almost to the door when she added, "I don't think it's anyone on the plane, though."

"Why not? They had the easiest way of getting to the pilots. And maybe hiding the *tjuringa.*"

"I know. But what were they going to do

when the fuel ran out and there was no one else to land the plane? The *tjuringa* wouldn't do them any good if they were splattered on the desert floor."

Mick was right. The whole thing just didn't add up.

Four pairs of eyes turned toward us as we jumped down from the wing.

"Find anything?" Gil asked.

"Just this," I said, handing him the thermos. "It's only half full. Both of the pilots could have drunk out of it."

John and his friend Gil sniffed the coffee and tasted a few drops to check for any signs of drugs, but they couldn't tell for sure. Mick and I went over to where the pilots still lay unconscious.

"How are they doing?" Mick asked.

"This one is stirring," Mrs. Fernandez said, pointing to Skip. "The other one hasn't moved."

"I hope they come around soon," Nancy said. "Maybe then we can get some answers. In the meantime, I think we should make a plan. How about if we build a signal fire? The authorities must be looking for us by now."

"I doubt it," I answered. "They probably just think we're a little late. The tour was due in Coober Pedy at one o'clock and, it's only a little before two o'clock now."

"Eventually someone will suspect there has been trouble and start a search," said Mr. Fernandez, while bouncing baby Anthony on his shoulder.

"It could take them a long time to find us," I told them.

"There has to be something we can do," Mrs. Fernandez said. She looked at Anthony, who had just fallen asleep on his father's shoulder. "We don't have much food or water. I didn't even bring a sweater in case it gets cold at night."

"Cold?" I asked. "The temperature hasn't dipped below seventy degrees since I've been here."

"That's on the coast," Mr. Fernandez said. "The desert can be broiling by day and freezing at night."

Just then, Skip groaned and opened his eyes. "Wh-wh-where am I," he said.

"Oh, thank goodness," Mrs. Fernandez said, walking toward him. She felt his forehead and gave him a drink of water. Then, Mr. Fernandez helped him sit up.

"I'm so dizzy," Skip said, lying back down. "What happened?"

"As near as we can tell, you were drugged," Nancy told him. "You and your copilot both."

Skip sat up and looked at Doyle, who was

64

still out. In an instant Skip became more alert. "B-But who landed the plane?"

"This young lady here," Gil said, clapping me on the shoulder. "She saved us twice."

Skip looked horrified. "Twice?"

All talking at once, they told Skip about our dive to certain death and then me landing the plane without fuel.

"You're a real hero," Skip said.

"I was just doing what I had to do," I said quietly. It felt weird to have everyone think I was a hero.

"We were just talking about what we should do," Nancy said.

"A rescue team will come for us," Skip said. "All we have to do is call on the radio."

"That's the problem," I said. "The wires on the radio have been cut."

"Cut?" Skip asked. "But who? Why?"

"We don't know," I answered. "But I do know we're at least one hundred miles off course, somewhere northwest of Flinders Ranges and Lake Eyre. The plane had been flying on autopilot for at least a half hour past Coober Pedy."

"Until it ran out of fuel," Mick said, "and took a nose dive."

Just then Doyle groaned and rolled over. "Ohh, my aching head," he moaned.

"Doyle," Skip said nudging him. "Are you all right?"

Doyle opened his eyes. "Except for a splitting headache and this dumb dream that we're camping out."

"We are camping out," Skip said. "Both of us have been unconscious for the past couple of hours. Dusty landed the plane, or else we would all be camping out in heaven."

Just like Skip, Doyle became instantly alert. He forced himself to sit up, and he stared at me. "You? You landed the plane?"

"That's right," Skip said. "She pulled us out of a dive and then landed without engine power." He told Doyle the whole story. The copilot just shook his head as if he couldn't believe it. Actually, I could barely believe it myself. I guess being terrified lets you do unbelievable things that you never thought you could.

"I don't know who did this," Doyle said, "who drugged us and left us in the sky, flying toward certain doom. But being stranded out here with night coming on isn't much better. There are snakes and dingoes and—"

"Well, what are we going to do about it?" Nancy asked. This started us all talking about making a plan. Some people started arguing. Skip stayed with us while Doyle went to see if he could fix the radio.

"I think we should start walking," John said, pointing back the way we came. "Civilization is back there somewhere."

"That's stupid," Gil said. "The search team will have better luck finding us if we stay by the plane."

"What's the use of staying here?" I said. "At least if we're walking, we'll be heading toward where we want to go."

"I think we should stay," Mick said. "The plane is bigger than us. The search team will find it easier."

"What if there is no search team?" Skip asked. "What if they spend all of their time looking on the other side of Coober Pedy? After all, that's where we were headed. Or maybe they'll think we went down in the mountains. They'll never think to search way out here."

"He's right," Mrs. Fernandez said. "Anthony can't survive out here for very long. We need to at least try to get back."

"I'm willing," Mr. Fernandez said. "But I think we should stay by the plane for a day, just in case they do come looking for us. The plane is shelter. It's going to be cold tonight."

"I don't have a coat," Mick said. "I vote for staying in the plane."

I pulled Mick aside and asked, "What happened to Mick, the outback expert? You're the one who's been hitting me with survival tips ever since I got to Australia."

"Well," she answered slowly. "I, uh, haven't really spent a lot of time in the outback. I mostly just sort of listened to my grandfather's stories about life out here. So, I really don't know any more than anybody else."

"Great," I said sarcastically.

The discussion died out after a while. People just wandered around the crash site, as if they were trying to get used to the idea that they might be stuck for a good long time—or forever. We were all lost in our own thoughts as we sat out of the sun in the shade of the scraggly trees. One by one, each person crawled into the plane to have a look around.

We gathered together what food and water we had and shared it. Nancy got her lunch from the plane and passed it around. Mr. Fernandez gave Anthony, who had been sleeping most of the time, a bottle of milk. I could tell the poor little guy was hot.

I actually found myself feeling sorry for him. I wondered how my parents would react if they were lost in the desert with their new baby. I mean, adults are stronger, hardier. But babies...I looked at Anthony's face, already beginning to turn pink in the sun. He was so weak and defenseless.

As the afternoon wore on and night began to close in, we waited—for what, we didn't know. I tried to keep track of everyone's movements, but I found myself getting drowsy from staring into the bright setting sun. Doyle and Skip spent a lot of the time in the plane, trying to fix the radio and figure out exactly where we were.

John passed me his water bottle. I drank from it and passed it to Mr. Fernandez. He took the bottle and said, "Dusty, I just want to thank you for saving us. Thank you for saving Anthony." He looked at him with loving eyes. "Because of you, he'll have a chance to grow up."

"*If* we ever get out of here," Gil said.

The pilots came back as we were talking. They didn't have any good news.

"I can't fix the radio," Doyle said. "It looks as if we're on our own."

About an hour later as darkness fell and the temperature dropped, Mr. Fernandez had built a campfire to give us a little light and heat. We had just started to pass around the little food we had left, when we heard a strange crackling sound. It was coming from the direction of the plane. Looking over, I saw that there seemed to be some kind of flickering light in the cockpit.

"What's that?" Skip asked. "Who's in there?"

I looked around quickly. We were all there.

Suddenly we saw a bright orange flame in the cockpit window. Mick put her hand on my shoulder.

"Dusty," she whispered in a voice that sounded unearthly. "My dream!"

"I know," I said, remembering the strange reflection that I had seen in her eyes.

Doyle took a step toward the plane. "I'll go fi—"

"NO!" Mick screamed, throwing herself at him and knocking him to the ground.

A second later, the plane exploded.

CHAPTER SEVEN
Following The Songline

"**G**ET down!" someone shouted as chunks of burning metal flew in all directions. Mick and I threw ourselves on the ground and covered our heads. Anthony screamed. I heard a woman crying, but I didn't dare lift my head to see who it was. The heat from the exploding plane was tremendous. I knew our decision to stay with the plane or go had just been made for us.

As dozens of smaller explosions ripped through the night, my mind was filled with questions. *Who could have done this? Why?* Airplanes don't explode by themselves when they're just sitting, out of fuel, in the middle of the desert.

I lifted my head to look at the burning plane. All that was left was a blackened skeleton, twisted and torn by the tremendous force of the explosion. Then I looked around me. Each one of us had been in the plane that afternoon, searching for clues, getting food, trying to fix the radio. Had anyone else— someone from the outside—been on the airplane, too?

But every face I could see, lit by the fire's hideous orange glow, reflected the same fear and shock.

After a while, the wind changed, blowing the smoke away from our meager camp.

"I think it's safe to get up," Skip cried. "Is everyone all right?"

We all stood up and walked toward the smoldering wreckage. Everyone began yelling at once. Accusations circled the group faster than a boomerang. Suspicion was so thick in the night air, you could have cut it with a knife.

"It has to be one of us," Doyle said, "because there's no one else here."

"Why do you think it's one of us?" Nancy demanded. "I think someone is watching us." She peered out into the solid blackness around us. "We're sitting ducks. They could strike again at any time."

Skip and Doyle started asking everyone questions about their backgrounds, why they were there, stuff like that. A few people protested, but most answered the questions.

"Look, what's the point of all this?" Mr. Fernandez asked.

Doyle turned suspicious eyes on him. "The point is, one of us may have tried to kill all the others," he said ominously. "And I'm trying to find out who it is!"

Mr. Fernandez grumbled something and turned away.

Doyle's eyes narrowed. "How about you?" he said to Nancy. "What are you doing? An American woman, all alone, in Australia?"

Nancy shrugged and said she was a librarian who liked to travel to the places she had read about. "Australia has always fascinated me," she explained. "This is my fourth time down under."

"Ah, we're not going to find out anything this way," Skip muttered.

As night closed around us, the conversation around the campfire slowly died. One by one, the passengers grew tired and fell asleep.

"I'm tired, Dusty," Mick said, leaning close to my ear. "But I'm too scared to go to sleep. I keep thinking about my parents. They must be worried sick about us. And they've probably called your parents by now, too."

I tried to see my parents, sitting in the living room back home, wondering if I were safe.

73

"Anything could happen," I told Mick.

Mick yawned. "I know." She stared at the flames, her eyes drooping.

"I know. Let's take turns keeping watch tonight," I said. "You sleep for an hour, and then I'll sleep."

"Okay. If you're sure."

"I'm not sleepy at all right now," I said.

"Be sure I wake up if anything happens."

I nodded, looking out past the campfire, into the starlit night. Embers from the still smoldering airplane cast an eerie glow on the empty, deserted landscape.

But maybe it wasn't deserted. Maybe it wasn't really empty. *Someone* could be out there, watching. The only person I felt I could trust was Mick. It was a strange feeling. A week ago, I would have thought my parents could protect me from anything. But now, here I was halfway across the world from them, and I had only myself, and Mick, to rely on. I looked over at her. I saw that she was already asleep.

My eyelids grew heavy as I fought to stay awake. I heard the deep breathing of the adults around me. I could see Anthony, snuggled into the arms of his mother and father. The look on his little face told me he didn't have the slightest idea that we were all in terrible danger. It seemed like a long time ago that I was that young, that trusting. For just a second I wished I could turn back the clock, be that little, have someone who would always take care of me.

But I pushed that thought out of my mind. I was fifteen. My time for being a baby was over. I knew I had to take care of myself—just as I had saved the plane from crashing. I didn't have time then to feel sorry for myself. I just did what I had to do without thinking about it. Maybe that's what it meant to be grown up.

I laid my head on my backpack, just to rest. I wondered about what they would think back home when they found out I had saved the plane and all the people. Would my instructor just skip the rest of my flying lessons and give me my license? I closed my eyes and saw myself getting medals and having my picture in all the papers and magazines. I'd meet the President, be on talk shows...

Applause. I could hear the applause of the TV audience. My parents were so proud. I was more important than the baby. People patted me on the back, clapped me on the shoulder...

It was Mick nudging my shoulder.

"Dusty!" she hissed. "Dusty, wake up! They were here while we were asleep!"

"W-what? Who was here?" I asked her, groggily.

"Whoever blew up the plane, I guess," she said.

"Huh?" I said sitting up.

The fire had died down. Dawn streaked the eastern horizon with faint stripes of pink and gold.

"It's almost morning," I whispered.

"I know. We slept all night. Look at the camp."

Everyone else was still sleeping, but the area was a bit messy. Everyone's bags were out of place and looked as if they'd been searched. The water bottle had been dumped, too. Immediately I reached for my backpack, but it hadn't been disturbed. Then I remembered that when I had fallen asleep, I had used it for a pillow.

"This is awful," I said. "I could kick myself for falling asleep."

"You couldn't help it, Dusty."

"Hey, everybody!" I called. "Wake up! We've been hit!"

We heard grumbles, followed by cries of surprise as each member of the group awakened and saw the mess around them.

"Hey! What's going on?"

"What happened?"

76

"Who did this?" Nancy asked, rubbing her eyes.

"I'll tell you," Doyle said roughly. "Look!" He pointed to where Gil and John had been sleeping. They were gone!

I gasped. "Do you think they did it?" I cried.

"They're gone, aren't they?" Doyle said.

"Well, that explains it then," Nancy said. "They were the ones all along. I was beginning to think that they were such nice guys."

"They *were* nice guys," Mr. Fernandez said. "I don't think they could have done this."

"Why else would they leave if they weren't guilty?"

"I don't know," Mrs. Fernandez said. "It just doesn't feel right. I think something has happened to them."

Doyle spat on the ground.

"Maybe they're around here somewhere," Mrs. Fernandez added. "I think we should look for them."

"Go ahead and look!" Nancy said in an angry voice. "But I guarantee you won't find anyone. They're gone! We had better all be thinking of ourselves and how we're going to get home."

"Well, I'm going to take a look," said Mr. Fernandez.

Doyle, Nancy, and Skip ignored him. They

had started arguing about which way was the shortest route to civilization.

"We'll come and look with you," I told Mr. Fernandez.

"I don't think they ran off," Mick said as we headed away from camp. "I think something happened to them."

"So do I, Mick," Mrs. Fernandez said. "We had a long talk with Gil and John yesterday. Even though they were aborigines, they weren't bushmen."

"That's right," her husband added. "They both worked in town, and neither one knew all that much about the outback."

"Maybe we should spread out, call their names," Mick said.

"I don't think so," I said. "I think we'd better stick together. Whatever happened to Gil and John could happen to us."

We decided to stick together. We called and looked for about an hour, but found no sign of the two men. There weren't even any footprints in the hard, rocky dirt.

We headed back to the wrecked plane, hot, tired, and disappointed. "I wonder if those three have figured out which way to go yet," Mr. Fernandez said.

"Probably not," his wife said. "I doubt any of us know the right way."

78

"If only we knew more about songlines," Mr. Fernandez said. "Remember our history lesson last week? We were teaching the kids at school that an aborigine could sing his way across Australia by using his songline."

"Uh, I know my songline," Mick said shyly. "At least, I know most of it. But I've never tried it out."

Mick looked at us.

"Well, we're sure in big trouble here," Mr. Fernandez said. "We don't have a clue about what to do. Whatever you know has to be better than what we know."

"I'm not sure," Mick answered. "Most everything I've learned has been from books. And it could be dangerous."

"Let me talk to her," I said, pulling Mick aside.

Mr. and Mrs. Fernandez walked on ahead of us. "Mick! You told me that you learned everything from your grandfather. You've been doing nothing but supplying me with tidbits about Australia since I got here. Now's not the time to start getting modest!"

"I don't know, Dusty," she replied. "What if something goes wrong? What if I can't remember it all, or if I can't control it?"

"Something's *already* gone wrong, Mick! We're stranded in the outback with no food and no water! What choice do we have?"

"Well, I'll give it a try."

Mick looked around and started humming. Her voice was weak at first, but it grew stronger as she gazed around trying to spot the old dreaming sites. "That might be a site over there," she said, pointing to a tall mound of rocks with a circle of trees around them.

"Okay, so start there and sing us home."

"It's not that easy, Dusty."

"Would it help if you looked at the *tjuringa?*" I whispered.

"I—I don't know," she answered. "It was so creepy last time. And I'm scared I'll make a mistake."

"If you don't try, we're goners for sure." I brought my backpack around in front of me and unzipped the pocket. Without taking the *tjuringa* out of the pocket, I unwrapped it.

With a quick glance around to make sure no one could see, Mick looked inside. As she ran her fingers along the intricately carved surface, I saw that she was going into the same kind of trance as on the airplane.

"Don't zone out, Mick," I pleaded.

"I'm here, Dusty," she said, her voice weird and low, like an ancient song. "But I can feel the power of the *tjuringa,* too. It's like I'm every red ant that ever lived and every red ant yet to be born."

This was so creepy it took all my strength not to scream out loud. The whole thing was weirder than any movie I'd ever seen!

"W-what does it say?" I asked. "Can you get us home?"

"No, not yet. But I think I can get us to water," Mick said. "It's not far from here."

Mick left the *tjuringa* in my backpack pocket and sang a few bars of a song. The words sounded like nonsense to me, but the music was, well, almost unearthly. She began walking in circles, reaching down every once in a while to touch a plant or a rock. Once she knelt to look at a lizard scurrying to its hole.

I rezipped my backpack and followed her as she wandered back toward the camp, singing softly all the while. Just before she reached the others, who were all staring at us, she veered to the south.

"Come on," I called. "Mick thinks she can sing us to where the water is."

"The sun is getting to her, isn't it? That's all we need! That girl's gone crazy!" Doyle said.

"I don't think so," Mrs. Fernandez said. "I think she's singing her songline."

"I've heard about that," Skip said. "It's kind

of like an internal map, isn't it?"

"Forget it!" Doyle said. "What we need is water."

"What we need is someone who knows how to get us out of here before the rest of us disappear or die of thirst!" Nancy shouted. "I've been listening to your ideas for hours and I haven't heard one good one yet!"

Doyle faced her, fury on his face. "And I suppose you think that following some crazy kid who doesn't have a clue about where she's going is a better idea?"

"She is an aborigine," Skip said. "Maybe you're wrong. Maybe she does have a clue."

"She said her grandfather taught her," Mr. Fernandez said. "What do we have to lose?"

CHAPTER EIGHT
Suspicion

A few weeks ago, if one of my friends back home had told me that I would be walking around in the Australian outback, following a girl singing a trail to a waterhole, I would have laughed. But I wasn't laughing now. I was too thirsty to laugh, not to mention too scared!

As we followed about ten yards behind Mick, I was keeping a close eye on the rest of the group. Which one of us was the guilty one? I didn't like Doyle. He kept wanting to follow too closely behind Mick. And maybe it was just my imagination, but I thought the jokes he was telling to Skip and the group to keep their spirits up were too much—as if he were trying too hard.

But he had been drugged, just like Skip. I couldn't really suspect him. I mean, even the stupidest criminal wouldn't drug himself when he was flying a plane.

What about Mr. and Mrs. Fernandez. Maybe they were the ones. Having a baby along would be the perfect cover. Maybe they weren't really teachers. They could be international jewel thieves looking for the opal labyrinths. Anthony might not even be theirs.

I looked over at the seemingly loving family. Could they be jewel thieves *and* kidnappers, too?

And then there were Gil and John. They had seemed like nice guys, but maybe Doyle was right. They were aborigines, and maybe they knew about the opals. They would know about using a *tjuringa*. They could be hiding out there someplace, just waiting for us to drop from thirst and exhaustion.

Nancy seemed like the least suspicious one. It was obvious she was just a tourist. I mean, how could anybody suspect a librarian? All they cared about was making kids be quiet!

"How long have we been walking?" said Patricia Fernandez, panting. "I'm not sure I can go much farther." The desert sun burned white hot in the sky overhead.

"Three hours," Nancy said hoarsely.

"Do you think I should go tell Mick we need to rest?" I asked.

"I can keep going," Nancy said. She seemed to have more energy than the rest of us. Maybe she thought of this as the greatest adventure of her life. After all, librarians must have pretty quiet lives.

"Dusty, could you please carry Anthony awhile?" Mr. Fernandez asked with a furrowed brow. "I'd better help Patricia."

"Uh, sure," I said, not really wanting to. I knew I had to help. His wife was getting weaker. But carrying a baby?

I flopped the sleeping Anthony up over my shoulder. He was even hotter than I was, if that was possible. His cheeks were bright red and his little puckered lips were chapped from the sun and wind. Poor little guy, I thought. As Mick had said earlier, I felt about ready to *do a perish*. That was Aussie slang that meant I was almost ready to pass out from lack of water. Anthony must have felt as bad or worse.

"I see a group of trees ahead!" Nancy said suddenly, pointing. "There must be a water-hole there."

I saw the trees, too. They didn't look very green or very healthy to me.

"At least we'll have some shade," Skip said. "I'm beginning to think Mick is leading us straight to nowhere."

But I could tell Mick wasn't paying atten-

85

tion to what we were saying. She just kept singing and touching things and looking around and singing some more.

When we reached the clump of trees, everyone slumped beneath them, happy for the little bit of shade. Mick sat next to me under a tree a little apart from the others. I could tell she was still singing silently in her head. Her eyes roved the landscape.

"Are you all right?" I asked.

"I think so," she said. "I need to look at the *tjuringa* again."

"Not here," I whispered back. "Someone might see us." We wandered away from the group and walked behind a little scraggly bush. Screened off from the others, Mick studied the *tjuringa,* once again tracing the outline of the symbols with her fingers. This time she concentrated on a curve that was sort of in the shape of a bush, with dots underneath.

"I think we're close," she said. "But I can't see it from here."

"See what?"

"The water. I know it sounds funny, but I can almost hear it gurgling underground." She dropped to her knees and put her ear to the ground. Then she sat back. "I wish—I wish—" she mumbled. "I wish I knew what all of these pictures inside my head meant."

Mick looked at me, tears welling up in her eyes and spilling over her dust-covered brown skin. She started to shake with sobs. I couldn't take my eyes off of the moist paths that her tears made or the look of sadness in her deep, brown eyes. I put my arm around her.

"All I know is that I've failed. I've led these people all over the desert, and for what? I can't find the water. We're probably going to die out here."

I found myself staring into Mick's eyes. Just like the day before, when I thought I saw the flames, maybe I could see something in them that would give us a clue.

There it was. Or was it? I couldn't be sure. Even though Mick's eyes were dark brown, for a second I thought I saw clear, bubbling, whitish-blue water. It seemed so real, almost like seeing a movie. Then it was gone.

"Mick," I said, afraid to look away. "I saw something in your eyes. I saw water."

"Sure you saw water," she said, blinking and brushing the tears from her face, smearing the dust. "I'm crying."

I shook my head. "No. Yesterday I saw fire. Today I saw a bubbling spring surrounded by rocks and red flowers." I got up and searched around the rocky area just beyond the bush.

"Red flowers?" she said, jumping up. "I'll help you look. If only you're right..."

Slowly we scoured the rough, brittle stones around us, our feet crunching through to the sandy dirt below. We looked for about ten minutes where we had been sitting. But the ground there was as dry as anywhere. I felt the sun beating down on my head and the sting of sunburn on my arms.

"This place is as dry as our bones are going to be in about two days," Mick said. She sniffed the air as a hot breeze blew by us.

"Maybe Skip was right," I answered. "Maybe the sun is getting—"

"Wait! Do you see that?"

"What?" I asked.

"Over there," she said, pointing ahead.

Mick ran toward a little ridge of reddish rock about 30 yards away. I ran after her. I saw her stop and look over the ridge. She had the strangest look on her face as she turned around to face me.

I caught up to her and peered over the ledge. Looking down I saw a carpet of red flowers, glowing in the sunlight, spilling over the rocks.

"Mick! Come on!" I shouted. "It's here!"

We both jumped down off the ledge.

"The ground is damp," she said, shoving

her hand in among the flowers. "Dig!"

As quickly as we could, Mick and I ripped apart the flowers looking for the source of the spring. The others heard our screams, and soon everyone surrounded us. Mick tore aside a final group of flowers, and there it was, bubbling and beautiful.

I almost cried.

Anthony did. He let out a thin, pitiful wail from his dry throat.

"Let the baby drink first," I heard myself say.

After we had drunk all that we could, we started out once more. The people were a little more cheerful after we found the water-hole, and they all watched Mick closely. If they hadn't believed in songlines and dreaming tracks before, Mick had sure given us something to think about—me included!

I trudged along, wondering exactly what to believe. Had I really seen the fire in Mick's eyes just before the plane blew up? Had I really seen the water? Was I imagining things, or had the initiation ceremony really got me tuned into some ancient aboriginal power?

"Where are we going now, Mick?" I asked, handing her the water bottle.

She took a little sip, which is all any of us could take since we were trying to save it.

"We're following the dreaming track to where it leads," she answered vaguely and went back to her singing.

"Another waterhole?" Skip asked.

"Maybe a whole string of them," Mick replied. "A string that will lead us to the sea."

"To the sea?" Nancy asked.

Mick didn't answer, but I looked at Nancy. She was the one who was most interested in Mick's singing.

Wisps of sand swirled in the slight breeze that stirred the scrubby plants in quiet relief after the heat of the day. We followed the sun as it set in the west, a great orange ball above the red dirt dunes.

Uphill.

"Do we have to go this way?" I whispered to Mick. "Wouldn't it be easier to walk around?"

Mick turned to me, her eyes glazed, her breathing short and panting. "I feel strange," she said. "I feel different. Kind of old and ancient."

"What do you mean old?"

"Not elderly or weak," she answered thoughtfully. "Old, like I'm a part of the earth, of history, of creation."

"You're scaring me, Mick. This dreaming track stuff is too weird.

"Listen," she said, staring into the distance,

humming her song. "Don't you think I'm scaring myself, too? All I know is that we have to go this way. It's the way the song is leading me." As the sun went down, we all followed her up the long, rippled side of a rocky ridge toward a row of sparse trees at the top.

The hill we had climbed was high and perfectly round. It looked kind of strange, almost too perfect to be a normal hill. It was hard to see in the dark, but it looked as if it could be flat on top. The moon rose behind us, bathing the ghostly gum trees in a white light that made their chalk-white trunks seem even more eerie.

Mick reached the top of the ridge first. She gasped and sat down hard, staring at the hilltop. I ran the last steps to her side, while the others lagged behind. "Are you hurt?"

"No, but look," she said.

There was no hilltop in front of us. Instead a giant bowl-shaped crater fell away from our feet. And in the center was what looked like hundreds of giant ant hills.

"Do you think it could be...?" I asked.

"I'm sure of it," she said, beginning to slide down the hill. "My songline and the *tjuringa* have led us directly to the secret red ant labyrinths! Dusty, this is horrible!"

CHAPTER NINE
The Mamu Held Death

"**W**H-WHAT do you mean, Mick? You wanted to come here, didn't you?"

"Yes, but not with everyone else," she said softly as the others began reaching the top of the hill. "I told you before that only red ant brothers and sisters are allowed to come here and return alive. I just know something terrible is going to happen, and it's all my fault!"

"You couldn't help it," I said, scooting down next to her. "The songline brought you here. You were just trying to help."

It was dark, but the moon lit the crater's interior with a pale, ghostly light. After we all stared in wonder at the bizarre place, we made our way down the curved sides. I couldn't imagine what had made this almost perfectly round crater. Then I remembered the words Mick had muttered in the plane about the sun falling to earth and burning its light into the ground to create the opals. Could it have been a meteor that created this place?

"I don't know what this big hole is," Skip said. "But it's protected from the wind. It's a good place to camp for the night.

"Look," Mrs. Fernandez cried. "I see some trees over there. I'll bet there's water."

We went to the spot and found a small pool of clear water. I saw the reflections of the round, bright moon and our seven tired faces.

Seven?

There should have been eight.

I looked around the circle of people. Skip, Nancy, Mick, the Fernandez family, and me. "Where's Doyle?" I asked.

Suddenly noticing he was missing, the others scanned the interior of the crater.

"He was right behind me when we were climbing up the outside of this bowl," Skip said in a panic. "What if something has happened to him? I'm going back to find him."

"Wait a minute, Skip," Nancy said. "What if Doyle was the bad guy all along and he's waiting back there to ambush you?"

"Not Doyle," Skip said. "I've known him for ten years. I can't leave him out here to die! I'm going back for him."

"I'll go with you," Mr. Fernandez offered.

"No, Joe, don't!" his wife said.

"I'll be all right," he assured her. "What can happen to two of us?"

"The same thing that happened to Gil and John," she told him. "We'll all go."

"She's right," Nancy said. "We'll all go."

We fumbled our way back along the rim of the crater searching for Doyle. For over an hour we looked, but in the dark we couldn't find a trace of him. Finally, Nancy found a branch and lit the end with a match. In the weak, flickering light we found seven sets of footprints in the sand, not eight.

"I just don't get it," Skip said. "I know we walked up the hill together. Why are my footprints here and not his?"

No one had an answer.

"We can't do anything more about this tonight," Nancy said. "It's getting cold. We had better build a fire and find a place to spend the night."

"I saw some wild tomatoes growing down there," Mick said. "And some *nyiri*. They taste kind of like potatoes. Help me gather some, Dusty. We can make a soup in Gil's billy can."

"Let's build a fire," Mrs. Fernandez said. "I don't want Anthony to get chilled."

Anthony had barely squawked or squeaked all day. I wondered if he was okay.

We all gathered wood, found a place to camp, and pitched in to get the fire going, even though we were worried about what had happened to Doyle. Who would be next? The feeling of helplessness, just waiting for something bad to happen and not being able to do anything about it, was gnawing at everyone.

Mick and I sat watching the flames, while everyone else went about their business. The baby was playing with a stick, putting it in his mouth. We watched him lying there, doing his baby thing as if we were in his living room, not lost out in the middle of the desert.

Nancy walked over and squatted down beside us. "Here. Let me finish up the dinner. You girls can take a break."

"Thanks," we said, getting up and walking a little distance away from the fire and up the side of the crater. We stood looking out at the dark horizon.

"It's all my fault," Mick said the minute we were out of earshot. "If I hadn't tried to use the *tjuringa,* Doyle wouldn't have disappeared. I wasn't sure if I really believed in the dreaming. But there's something really creepy going on." She looked at me, her eyes big with fear. "Dusty, do you think the curse on those who enter the red ant dreaming track is coming true?"

"I don't know," I said, trying to calm her. "I think there could be a natural explanation for everything. I have a feeling someone very human is behind all of this. They're sneaky, that's for sure. But they'll make a mistake before long. Just wait and see."

I heard my own words, trying to convince Mick that there had to be a normal explanation for what was going on. But I wasn't sure if I really believed them myself.

After a few minutes, Mick said, "There's something else I have to tell you, Dusty. I saw something else today."

I saw that Mick's hands were shaking. I knew it wasn't from the cold. It wasn't that cold.

"I saw a *mamu*, actually two, side by side."

"W-what's a *mamu?*"

"They're ancient evil spirits who have always preyed on my people. They were standing on the ridge of this bowl, motioning for me to enter. One held handfuls of opals...," she said, her voice trailing off.

"And the other *mamu?*"

"The other held—death."

"Death?" I said, almost gasping. "What do you mean? What kind of death?"

Mick thought for a moment. "The *mamu* held a bag. The inside was kind of like an empty hole," she said. "Like a bottomless pit. I knew it meant death."

I didn't know what to think. Could it really be happening to me, a normal kid from New York? Could I really be stuck in the middle of a supernatural nightmare that I couldn't wake up from? Had Mick gone over the deep end from fear, believing the legends and campfire stories her grandfather had told her? I didn't know. I needed time to think.

"Dusty," she said. "I just want you to know that if we don't make it out of this alive, I've really liked knowing you. Even though we've known each other mostly from writing letters, you've been a really good friend."

I put my arm around her and said softly, "We'd better be getting back before they think something has happened to us, too."

CHAPTER TEN
Into The Labyrinth

"LOOK at them, Dusty," Mick said later after we had eaten the soup. "They're beautiful, even though they scare me. It's almost as if they're glowing from inside." The moon bathed the ant hills in a supernatural silver light.

"Do you think we should try to go inside the labyrinths?" I asked her.

"I don't know," Mick answered. "I only know the part of the song to get us here. I don't know the melody which would take us safely through the labyrinths."

"Listen, maybe they aren't ant hills at all," I said. "Maybe they're just strange rock formations. Maybe it's the night that makes them look so weird. In the morning they'll look perfectly normal."

But Mick just shook her head and stared

into the fire. "If they aren't the red ant laby-rinths, why would the *mamus* be here?"

It looked as though she really believed that she saw them. I knew it would not do any good to try to convince her that they were just her imagination—not tonight anyway.

Mick yawned. My eyelids drooped as we sat, staring into the fire. Neither the strange place we were in nor the threat that some-thing else might happen could make me keep my eyes open.

"Maybe we'd better try to get some sleep," I suggested.

Mick yawned again. "One of us should stay awake and keep watch," she said. She looked around. Mr. and Mrs. Fernandez and the baby were already asleep. Nancy was dozing on the other side of the fire next to Skip.

"I can't keep my eyes open," I said. "I want to, but it feels as if something is closing them for me."

"I know what you mean," Mick said, yawn-ing again and lying down. "I feel so tired, so—dog—tired." Her head dropped to the ground, and she was asleep.

I joined her in about a half a second. I don't know how long I was asleep, but I had strange dreams that night. I dreamed about soldiers marching around the fire and into endless corridors and passageways. Sounds filled my ears, but I couldn't tell whether the marching sounds were coming from my dream soldiers or from inside my own head.

As I gradually started to wake up, I became aware of my aching head and a strange tingling all over my body. I tried to make myself go back to sleep. But the sound of a baby crying penetrated into my dreams. Anthony!

"Mick?" I whispered. "It's dark. Where are we?"

"Dusty," she called softly. "I don't think we're outside anymore. Don't move until we figure out where we are."

I couldn't have moved even if I wanted to. My heart felt as if it was wrenched out of my chest. Raw fear closed around my throat. "We're inside—the ant hills!" I said.

"Anthony is with me," Mick said. "He's lying on my arm. He's okay."

"My eyes are starting to get used to the darkness," I said. "But my skin feels all creepy-crawly, and I get dizzy when I look at the walls. It's like they're moving."

MOVING!

"Aarrgghh!" I screamed hysterically. "Ants! Ants all over me!" I started madly brushing at my face and clothes. I jumped up and danced around, trying to knock them off. I couldn't breathe, my panic was so overpowering.

There were too many of them!

They were huge, the biggest ants I had ever seen. Their plump, red bodies were everywhere—my eyelids, my lips, my ears. I could feel each foot, each searching antenna. It was only a matter of time before they all started to bite. My panic grew worse and worse. To lose my mind would have been a relief!

"Don't slap at them, Dusty," Mick said. "Be careful where you step."

I couldn't talk. The only sound I heard from my throat was a moaning that didn't sound human.

"Dusty, they're not biting us!" Mick said, standing up next to me.

I couldn't believe how calm she was. But suddenly I realized it was true.

"They know who we are!"

"I think you're right. They haven't bitten me," I said.

"And I don't think they will," Mick said. "Look, they're leaving me now. You too."

There was an eerie glow inside the labyrinth, and it illuminated Mick's face. I watched her stand there quietly while streams of red ants flowed off of her and Anthony and onto the floor of the tunnel we were standing in.

It took every ounce of willpower I had to stand still and let the ants march off me. I could feel them everywhere—in my hair, on my face, in my clothes.

My insides churned. I closed my eyes and tried not to be sick until the last insect had jumped off of my foot. When I opened my eyes, the ants were gone. The tunnel was empty and the only sound was the sound of millions of ant feet—marching to an ancient rhythm.

Mick handed Anthony to me and put both hands on the wall. I watched her. Her head tilted to the side, and she seemed to be listening intently. Was she listening to the sound of the ants, feeling them through the vibrating walls? Suddenly she dropped to the floor and traced the patterns of the ant tracks with her finger.

"I have an idea," she said. "Hand me the *tjuringa.*"

I reached down and felt around for my backpack. Anthony clung to my neck as I searched frantically.

"It's not here!" I cried. "Whoever dragged us in here must have taken it."

"Oh no! I was going to use the *tjuringa* to help me sing the songline from beginning to end as we traced the markings on the floor. I thought the song might lead us out."

"But can't you sing the whole song without the *tjuringa?*" I asked.

"No. We can only get so far. The lost *tjuringa* is the missing piece."

"But what would happen?" I asked.

"It could mean total destruction—of the labyrinths, of the whole continent. I—I don't even want to think about it. And if whoever stole the *tjuringa* tries to sing the songline and sings it wrong, then everything about the red ant dreaming track could disappear. Including us."

"Do you think whoever has the *tjuringa* knows what could happen?" I asked.

"I don't know. But we can't take the chance. We've got to get it back somehow. But I'll tell you one thing the thief knows," she added.

"What's that?"

"That he was leaving us here to die."

"But who could it be, Mick? Do you—"

Suddenly, without warning, the sound of ants marching filled the walls around us. What had been a distant rumbling was now incredibly loud. What had made them start to stampede?

"Where are they? What's going on?" I said.

"Something is happening," Mick said.

"Something bad!"

CRACK!

The sound exploded in the corridor around us. Anthony screamed in terror. We both turned to see a huge gash opening in the wall next to us. Then the passageway began to shake. It was just a small vibration at first, no louder than the sounds of the marching ants. Then the shaking grew. Dirt fell from the ceiling onto our heads. It filled the passageway with a veil of reddish dust.

Then, in the distance, my ears picked out another sound. I strained to catch it.

"Do you hear that?" I whispered, my fear growing.

"Oh no!" Mick cried. "I can't believe it! This can't be happening! It could mean the end of everything!"

CHAPTER ELEVEN
A Monster's Face

"**I**T sounds like a man's voice," I whispered. "And he's singing the songline."

"Come on," Mick said. "We have to sing it before he does, before he destroys us all!"

"Hang on, Anthony," I said.

He smiled. Even in the dim light I could see it. He reached up and touched my face. He was counting on me—on us.

Mick dropped to her knees again. She looked up at me. I knew she was afraid—deathly afraid—of singing it wrong.

"I trust you, Mick," I said. "I know you can do it. You sing it, I'll follow. And Mick, one more thing."

"Huh?"

"Sing fast. Anthony's too young to die."

She grinned. "Right, mate. So are we."

Mick's fingers shook as she traced the an-

105

cient red ant carvings on the floors and walls of the labyrinth. Then, her voice quivering from fear, she began the song. From the beginning.

She began to walk. I followed Mick, deeper and deeper into the labyrinth, as the walls crumbled around us. Every now and then, between crashes, I heard the man's voice singing the strange words, somewhere in the strange light.

Anthony clung to my neck, whimpering softly. Poor guy, I thought. He didn't ask for this. A warm bottle, a dry diaper, that's all he cared about. But what of his parents? What if they were dead? What would Anthony do then? I had a totally strange thought. *My* parents were having a baby. Maybe they would take Anthony in, too—like having twins. I could even help take care of him.

I dodged a heavy chunk that fell from the ceiling.

What was I thinking? One baby was going to be bad enough. But I didn't like the thought of Anthony being all alone in the world.

The crashing of rock grew louder, filling my ears. We stumbled on the fallen debris, but Mick pressed on, her eyes closed, her fingers following the song on the wall. She would hesitate at corners and intersections.

But somehow she knew which way to go.

The voice grew louder, then softer as we walked. We walked for at least a half hour. A couple of times I thought we had gone the wrong way for sure and were hopelessly lost. But then it seemed to get a little lighter, and the singing became louder again.

"Where are we going, Mick?"

"I don't know," she answered. "Wherever the song leads us."

Then suddenly, the tunnel we were in opened up into a large room, a cavern at least the size of a football field, dripping with water on all sides. It was the most beautiful place I had ever seen. Light bounced off of the walls, creating millions of rainbows. The light and beauty of the cavern almost blinded me.

As my eyes adjusted to the light, I realized that the walls were not wet with water. They were studded with opals of every shape, size, and color. It was unbelievable!

But in the center of the cavern, in front of a low flat table, stood Doyle, the *tjuringa* raised in his hands.

"Hurry!" I said. "We have to stop him!"

Mick stepped out into the cavern, still singing softly.

Doyle must have heard her, because he turned and pointed the *tjuringa* at us. He shouted something I couldn't understand. Suddenly a huge section of the wall split apart and crashed in front of me, separating Anthony and me from Mick.

"Dusty!" Mick screamed.

"I'm all right," I called back through the rubble. Behind me another section tumbled down, sealing the passageway—a passageway that had become my tomb.

"I'll dig you out," Mick yelled from the other side.

"No, go on! There isn't much time."

"I won't leave you," she cried.

"You have to. Get to Doyle. Only you can stop him!"

Darkness closed around me. Behind me I felt the rocks that filled the passageway. In front of me, I touched another wall of rock. Anthony and I were trapped between two cave-ins. And the air was already becoming hard to breathe. I could hear faint sounds of singing. I began to wonder if they were just inside my head and whether this was all a dream—a bad dream I could wake up from whenever I wanted.

Dizzy, Getting dizzy.

I had never felt so alone in all my life. At any minute, I expected the rest of the corridor to cave in, and we'd be buried alive.

It would be so easy just to sit down and let it happen. Who would miss me anyway?

A loud crash somewhere startled me. I must have been almost unconscious.

It's hopeless. Why struggle against it?

Then Anthony cooed and reached up to tug on my hair. I knew that I had to try, for his sake.

"Come on, Anthony. We're going to get out of here!"

I shifted him onto my other hip and started digging with my free hand. I began at the top and pulled the rocks down, letting them tumble behind me. I felt the sticky warmth of my own blood on my fingers, but I kept on digging.

Just when I thought I couldn't dig anymore, a crack of light appeared at the top of the pile. I pulled another rock, and a gust of fresh air filled our tomb.

"Anthony," I cried. "We're going to make it out of here."

Working frantically, hysterically, ignoring my bleeding hand, I yanked out rock after rock. I could see the cavern. I could see Mick and Doyle. I could hear her shouting at him, telling him to stop.

"Okay, old boy," I said. "Out you go." I pushed Anthony through the hole that I had made, and I wiggled out behind him. "We're coming, Mick!"

I ran toward them with Anthony bouncing along under my arm.

"It's no good," Mick was telling Doyle. "Only those who have been initiated can gaze upon the opals and live."

"Hogwash!" Doyle replied, his eyes glazed. "I've lived my whole life for this moment. No little girl and no idiotic superstition is going to stop me now! I'm warning you, leave me alone so that I can concentrate."

As I got closer, I saw that the long table was really a series of *tjuringas,* like a puzzle pieced together above the shining floor. Doyle held the last piece above a space of the exact same shape.

Desperately I tried to think of a way to stop him from putting the last piece in its place.

"Hey, Doyle! Tell us how you did it?" I yelled as I reached them. "You must be a genius. No one else has found the labyrinths." I paused. "Except for Wild Joe—and everyone knows what happened to him."

He lowered the *tjuringa* and stopped singing. The look in his eyes made him seem like a wild animal—or something even worse.

He laughed hysterically. "Wild Joe was my father! But he was stupid. He left the *tjuringa*

110

home with me when he went off to sing the songline. For the past 20 years I've continued his search. I won't meet the same end!" he said.

I reached Mick and grabbed her arm.

"All these years, I've searched. I've studied. I've found other treasures, but this is the best. This is my crowning achievement! It's mine! All mine!" he said with his wicked laugh.

"And you were bringing Wild Joe's *tjuringa* on the plane, the one we found?"

"That's right. I figured you had found it and it was in your backpack, little girl, because I had searched everyone else's stuff. I found it this evening when you were asleep."

"But Doyle, how did you expect to get here if the plane crashed?" I asked. "I mean, why did you drug yourself?"

For a moment Doyle's eyes flickered and returned to normal. "I didn't drug myself. I doped Skip's coffee. I don't know how I took any myself."

He shook his head, his eyes taking on their greedy gleam once again. "But that doesn't matter now. The glory is mine." He turned to face the songline once again, ready to insert the last *tjuringa* in its place.

I leaned close to Mick and whispered, "I'll keep him talking. You sneak around there behind him."

She nodded.

"You were really smart to fool all of us, Doyle," I said, taking a step toward him. "Tell me, how did you get rid of all of the others."

"Stupid fools," Doyle said. "They must've run off by themselves. They won't last much longer and neither will you. You're going to be buried alive, and I'm going to have all of the opals."

"But why are you singing the song backward. Don't you know that you'll destroy the labyrinths?"

"Of course I know I'm singing it backward. I've got to un-sing it to reveal the treasure underneath. The opals are buried beneath the surface. All I have to do is get rid of all these ant hills, and then I will stake a mining claim. With all this for myself, I'll be the richest man on earth!"

He gave me an insane look and reached out his arm to place the last *tjuringa* in its spot. He started to sing the tune I now knew so well.

"No!" Mick shouted, lunging at him from behind. The tjuringa went flying out of his hand. I set Anthony down and ran to help.

But Doyle fought like a madman. He flung us aside. We rushed him again.

"Get the *tjuringa!*" Mick yelled as she yanked on his hair.

I grabbed for it, but Doyle was faster. He swung his arm at me and sent me flying. I scrambled back up to tackle him again, but suddenly he grabbed Anthony and put his hand up to stop us.

"Stop! Unless you want something to happen to the baby!"

We froze. Anthony's tear-filled eyes met ours, but he didn't cry. Doyle held Anthony over his shoulder and began to sing the songline once again.

"Doyle, please put the baby down," I pleaded. "He's never done anything to you. We'll leave you alone. We promise. Just put Anthony down."

He wasn't listening. He was deep into the songline as the cavern tumbled about us.

"Please!" I screamed. "Don't hurt the baby! Put him down!"

"Yes, Doyle," a woman's voice said from behind us. "Put the baby down."

"Nancy!" I shouted, looking around.

She aimed a pistol at Doyle and walked toward our group. Slowly Doyle lowered Anthony to the rock floor, keeping his eyes fixed on the gun in Nancy's hand.

"Thank goodness," Mick said. "You've got

to stop him." I moved to pick up Anthony, but Nancy waved me away.

"Stop him?" she said. "No, I don't think so. I thought his plan sounded like a good one. So I'll let him continue. The only difference is that I'll take the opals!" She pointed the gun at Doyle's head and ordered, "Keep singing!"

"But, Nancy—" I began.

"Shut up!" she said. "You two must not have had much soup. You didn't stay out as long as the others."

"So *you're* the one who drugged my food," Doyle said.

"That's right. And I would have landed the plane if Dusty here hadn't saved me the trouble!"

"And you got rid of Gil and John?" Mick asked.

"That was easy," she said with a laugh, "because Doyle was nice enough to take care of them for me. Drugging your soup last night was easy, too. You didn't even notice that I didn't eat with you."

"Where are the others?" I asked.

"It doesn't matter," she answered, all the time keeping her gun trained on Doyle. "I'm the only one who is going to survive this little adventure. I've researched this place for years, and now that I've found it, no one is going to stand in my way. You'd better sing, Doyle, if you know what's good for you. And if you're really nice, I might even cut you in."

Doyle began singing. But as he got past the *tjuringa,* he became confused. No longer was he singing the songline backward. He was mixing the pieces up, singing it out of order. Having a pistol pointed at his head must have scared him out of his mind.

"You better get it right, you fool!" Nancy shouted. She cocked the trigger on the pistol. Mick and I backed away and hid behind a boulder.

"What are we going to do?" I whispered, keeping an eye on Anthony, who was crawling around in the sand.

"We have to do something," Mick said. "Or we'll all be killed. We—"

CRRAACCKK!

The sound was deafening, louder than a gunshot, louder than a thunderbolt. It split the air around us. Without warning, the ground opened up in front of the *tjuringa* table, throwing Nancy and Doyle down.

The yawning crevice filled the cavern with a blinding, white light. We were stunned speechless.

"The opal grotto!" Mick finally said. I couldn't believe my eyes. We were seeing the

115

legendary room. Except it wasn't a legend. It was real!

That's when I noticed Anthony. He was sitting right on the edge of the gaping crevice, playing with his toes. He didn't seem to notice what was going on around him. He was in his own little world. But I saw that if he moved even an inch, he would fall into the grotto.

When Nancy and Doyle recovered their senses, they crawled to the edge of the grotto and peered down inside. The light from the opal grotto shined up and lit their evil, smiling, distorted faces with a ghoulish glow. They were the smiles of pure greed.

"This is it," Nancy said. "And it's all mine!"

"No, it's mine!" Doyle shouted. "I found it. I've worked my whole life for this moment. I'm not going to let you take it away from me!"

Doyle reached out and grabbed for her gun. They struggled like wild animals in a fight to the death—pulling, tugging, ripping—on the very edge of the crevice.

"We have to get Anthony," I said.

"Now, while they're busy fighting," Mick said.

We crawled carefully toward the edge, calling to him softly. "Anthony. Don't move, baby. We're coming."

Anthony turned his head to look at us, his baby features illuminated by the light from the opal grotto. In contrast, Anthony's smile was pure, simple and innocent. He was happy to see me.

"Come on, Anthony," I said. "Come to Dusty. We'll go for another ride."

He reached his hand toward me. As our fingers were about to touch, another loud sound rang out.

CRACK!

This time I knew it was a gunshot.

As if in slow motion, I saw Doyle jerk and Nancy step back as he started to tumble into the grotto. His hand reached for a rock and grabbed onto it. Nancy turned to us, her face contorted, hideous with rage and greed, a monster's face. She raised her gun, aiming at us from not more than twenty feet away.

CHAPTER TWELVE
The Secret Of The Tjuringa

"TAKE cover!" I heard Mick shout, but I was already flat on the ground partly hidden behind a rock. Another shot rang out through the noise of the rumbling rocks around us. But it went wide, ricocheting off the ceiling.

I raised my head just an inch. In what seemed like hideous slow-motion, I watched as Doyle pulled himself partly up over the ledge. Nancy was watching us and didn't see him. He reached for her leg. Even though I knew she had tried to kill us, somehow I just couldn't let her die. I started to scream out a warning to her to look out for Doyle.

But I was too late. Before my horrified eyes, Doyle grabbed her leg and twisted her to the ground. As she tried to jerk away, she made him lose his balance. But he didn't lose his grip on Nancy's leg.

Together they fell, screaming, into the blinding white light of the grotto far below.

The walls of the cavern shook violently. The floor beneath us quaked, and the ledge began to split away and fall into the grotto. I grabbed for Mick's arm to catch my balance.

In the next second, I saw Anthony begin to tumble toward the edge. His baby hands uselessly gripped the dust around him.

"Anthony!" I hollered. "No!"

Then I leaped. I'm not quite sure how I did it, but it felt as if I were flying. In one giant lunge, I grabbed for his leg just as he fell over. He dangled over the edge, but I held on as tight as I could. *Please don't let me drop him,* I prayed.

Just then, the ground shifted again, and I felt the ledge tilt beneath me. I started sliding toward the edge.

"Help! Mick!" I yelled. "Help me!"

And then I felt the most wonderful feeling. Mick grabbed onto my legs and pulled. I don't know where she got the strength. But she pulled Anthony and me back from the edge of certain death.

"We have to get out of here!"

"It's too late!"

"It can't be too late," I said. "Come on."

Mick scampered across the shaking cavern floor to the *tjuringa* table. She looked quickly at the remaining *tjuringas* and then turned to me, bracing herself against the stone.

"I think I've got it," she said.

"The whole thing?"

"It's already in my head. I can't explain it."

"Then go for it, mate!" I yelled at the top of my voice.

Mick sang. I followed, carrying Anthony. I could hear Mick clearly over the shaking and the cracking of the ancient walls. We sprinted through the open corridors, following where the songline led Mick. I don't think I ever ran faster than I did then. I knew that each moment could have been my last. Any second, I expected to be buried alive in an avalanche of sand and stone. But the walls held. I had said I didn't really believe in the songline. But then and there, I had the strong feeling that Mick was holding the walls together with her song.

After what could have been minutes or hours of running, running for our lives, we burst suddenly into the night air. As we fell to the desert floor in relief under the starfilled sky, the hill where we had just been collapsed in on itself! Then, one by one, all except one of the other hills at the dreaming site collapsed, too.

Out of the opal grotto deep in the ground, the incredible light still shined, piercing the black sky with a pure-white column of unbelievable power. It probably could have been seen on Mars! But as we watched, the light began to fade. It must have meant that the earth was collapsing around the grotto, sealing it up again—maybe this time forever.

We rested on the ground, trying to catch our breath, as the ground continued to tremble and move. Finally I spoke about what I knew was on our minds.

"The others, Mick," I said. "If they were taken to caves, too, there's no way they could have survived this."

"I know."

I looked at the rubble around us where the majestic ant hills used to stand. "It's too horrible to think about, Mick, all this destruction, all this—death." I hugged Anthony, smoothing his baby-fine hair. "I'm sorry, baby. This looks like the end of the line."

As the last of the light from the opal grotto faded out, we found ourselves in darkness again. The vast outback was lit only by the stars and the full moon. I felt as if we were the only three people on earth. Why had we even tried to escape from the collapsing labyrinths? To die of thirst out here in the desert? It had never looked more hopeless. I started to cry.

Mick put her arm around me. But she knew how hopeless it was. There was nothing she could say.

After we had sat there for a while, we heard another loud cracking sound. We knew it well. It was the sound of rocks splitting in two, almost right under us.

"Look out, Dusty! Here comes another one!"

We jumped back, afraid we would be sucked into another underground deathtrap. The last remaining ant hill cracked open right in front of us. In the moonlight, we were able to just make out what looked like a small open space, like a little room.

"Dusty! Look!"

In the moonlight, I could barely see the outlines of bodies.

"They're here!" Mick yelled. "They're all in here."

"Are they—alive?" I was afraid to look.

We ran to the destroyed ant hill.

"Yes!" Mick yelled. "They're alive!"

It only took us a few minutes to untie them—Patricia and Joe Fernandez, Gil, John, and Skip. When I handed Anthony to his parents, their eyes filled with tears.

They all jabbered at once, asking so many questions that we couldn't answer them all.

"How—?"

"You saved us—"

"What happened? We thought we were goners," Skip said.

Mick and I explained how Doyle and Nancy had each been working to get us out of the way. We told them about how they fell to their deaths in the labyrinth.

Skip shook his head. "My old friend Doyle. I can't believe he would leave us here to die."

"And Nancy seemed so nice," Patricia said. "She turned out to be bad, too, drugging the soup and dragging us into the caves, almost making the plane crash."

"But I don't understand. What were they looking for out here?" Joe asked.

Op—"

"Oh, we don't know, she's trying to say," Mick interrupted me. She shot me a quick look that said *Shhh!*

"But how did you guys get here?" Mick quickly asked Gil and John, changing the subject. "We thought you were long gone."

"Doyle knocked us out back by the plane and hid us inside the burned wreckage," Gil explained. "When we came to, we got untied and followed your trail. But he ambushed us again just as we reached this place."

Patricia said. "I'm just glad it's over."

Joe turned to us with a questioning look in his eyes. He looked as if he suspected there was more to the story than we were letting on. "What I want to know is where were you all of this time? How did you get out—?"

"Listen!" Skip yelled. "What's that sound?"

We all strained our ears.

"It's more rumbling in the ground," Patricia said.

"No, I don't think so," Skip replied.

"Look, over there!" Joe cried. "There's a helicopter coming!"

We all jumped up and started screaming like crazy people. I waved my arms until they hurt. I think it was the happiest moment of my life when the big military helicopter landed close by and the pilot ran out to greet us.

"Are you folks from the Opal Tours charter?" the man asked.

"What's left of us," Joe said. "The copilot and one of the passengers were killed."

"Come on," he shouted over the roar of the engines. "The safest place is in the air right now. You folks have survived being in the epicenter of the biggest earthquake Australia has seen since 1906."

"Earthquake?" I asked.

"That's right," the pilot answered. "And the epicenter has been tracked to this very spot."

My jaw dropped like a stone. I stared at Mick.

"We were about to give up on you," the pilot said. "But we followed your signal."

"Signal?" Patricia asked. "What signal?"

The pilot laughed. "The light you shot up into the sky. That is some flashlight you've got! I'll bet they could see it all the way to Adelaide."

"Light?" Joe asked me as we followed the pilot to the chopper. "Do you know anything about a light?"

I shrugged my shoulders and looked at Mick. "No," I answered. "We didn't shine any light."

As we climbed into the helicopter, the other pilot said, "The newspapers are calling it the Great Australian Earthquake."

Mick and I were silent. I knew now that she was right. We couldn't tell the whole story. It would mean the destruction forever of the ancient red ant dreaming site, the opal grotto, and everything. It was a secret we had to keep. The only other ones who knew the secret were Nancy and Doyle. And they'd never tell, now.

I knew the others were confused about what had really happened. But they had never seen the ants or the opals, or heard the *tjuringa* sung in the labyrinth. It was better that they didn't know.

As the helicopter lifted into the night, I gazed sadly down at the huge pile of jumbled rocks that had once been the red ant dreaming site. The earthquake—or whatever it was—had destroyed their home.

"Don't feel bad, Dusty," Mick whispered. "I know they're going to rebuild it. I don't know what really happened down there, but we've seen something that no one else has ever seen and survived. Everything's going to be all right again."

I nodded. The secret was safe with us. Then I said to her, "I was just wondering something myself. How *did* we get separated from the others?"

"I don't know, mate. But I think some things are better not to know."

Just then Anthony gurgled and reached out to me from across the aisle.

"Dusty, we really owe you so much," his mother said. "I don't think we can ever thank you enough. But we were wondering if you'd be willing to be Anthony's godmother." She held him out to me.

"I—I don't know what to say," I said, taking Anthony. "Sure, I'd be honored."

"I think he likes you," Joe said.

"You're all right, too, Anthony," I told him as I lifted him over into my lap. I turned to Mick. "Hey! I guess I'm going to be a godmother *and* a big sister! I think I'm really going to like that!"

The three of us together looked out at the ruined dreaming site. "Look, Anthony," I whispered. "Mick says everything's going to be all right again. And it will be—with you, with me, and down there."

I looked at Mick's reflection in the window. She was smiling. I smiled, too, but we both had tears in our eyes—tears of happiness.

About the Author

CINDY SAVAGE lives with her family in a big house on a small farm in northern California. She published her first poem in a local newspaper when she was six years old and has been hooked on reading and writing ever since. She's the author of more than 20 books for children and young adults. In her spare time, she plays with her family, reads, does needlework, bakes bread, and looks after her garden.

Traveling has always been one of her hobbies. As a child, she crossed the United States many times with her parents, visiting Canada and Mexico along the way. Now she takes shorter trips to the ocean and the mountains. She gets her inspiration from the places she visits and the people she meets.

Among her many books for Willowisp Press are *Project: Makeover, Caught in the Act,* two adventures—*Cave of the Living Skeletons* and *The Curse of Blood Swamp*—and the Forever Friends series.